**She remembered the first time she'd met him, a cowboy in faded jeans.**

His smile had put her teenage heart into overdrive. She'd spent the next year wrapped in daydreams of a guy that she'd been afraid to talk to.

In search of her aunt, she finally spotted Janie, standing at the edge of the crowd at the rodeo. Next to her was a man Willow didn't recognize. This man wore a bent-up cowboy hat. The strong angles of his jaw proved he was no longer a kid.

Willow joined her aunt and Clint Cameron. He took off his hat, revealing sandy blond hair, a five-o'clock shadow and a slow, easy grin.

He wasn't a gangly teen anymore. And her heart still did that funny dance when he smiled at her. As a girl, she hadn't known what to do with that reaction. Now she carefully tamped it down, because she didn't need complications to her already complicated life.

**Books by Brenda Minton**

Love Inspired

*Trusting Him*
*His Little Cowgirl*
*A Cowboy's Heart*

## *BRENDA MINTON*

started creating stories to entertain herself during hour-long rides on the school bus. In high school she wrote romance novels to entertain her friends. The dream grew and so did her aspirations to become an author. She started with notebooks, handwritten manuscripts and characters that refused to go away until their stories were told. Eventually she put away the pen and paper and got down to business with the computer. The journey took a few years, with some encouragement and rejection along the way—as well as a lot of stubbornness on her part. In 2006, her dream to write for Steeple Hill Books Love Inspired line came true.

Brenda lives in the rural Ozarks with her husband, three kids and an abundance of cats and dogs. She enjoys a chaotic life that she wouldn't trade for anything—except, on occasion, a beach house in Texas. You can stop by and visit at her Web site, www.brendaminton.net.

# A Cowboy's Heart
## Brenda Minton

Steeple
Hill®

Published by Steeple Hill Books™

STEEPLE HILL BOOKS

**Steeple Hill®**

Recycling programs
for this product may
not exist in your area.

ISBN-13: 978-0-373-81395-7
ISBN-10: 0-373-81395-3

A COWBOY'S HEART

www.SteepleHill.com

**Printed in U.S.A.**

The Lord is my strength and my song, He has become my salvation: He is my God, and I will praise Him. My father's God, and I will exalt Him.

—*Exodus* 15:2

To my sister Ellen Benham and my brother-in-law Gary. This is dedicated to you, for computers, for weekends away and for friendship.

To Doug and the kids, because they love me, even during a deadline crunch.

And of course to Melissa Endlich and Janet Benrey. Without their encouragement and belief in my stories, I'd still be piling unpublished manuscripts in the closet.

To faithful and true friends, strong women all, without whom my phone batteries would always be charged, and I'd be a blob of insecurity. Thank you for listening, for reading and for always being there for me. Steph, Shirlee, Angela, Tonya, Dawn, Barbara, Betty, Janice, Lori W and Keri.

For my number-one fan, Denise Foster Dickens. And Josie, for dinner, and for being the most amazing neighbor ever.

To the girls at the Marionville, MO, library for support and encouragement.

A deep debt of gratitude to Janet McCoy, for answering questions and sharing stories.

To all of the women who struggle, hold on to faith and never give up. Especially to my new sister-in-Christ, Shirley. You are strong and beautiful.

## Chapter One

Country music crackled from aging PA speakers that hung from the announcer's stand next to the rodeo arena, and dozens of conversations buzzed around Willow Michaels. It was hard to discern one sound from another, and harder still to know if the queasy nervousness in her stomach was due to her bulls about to compete, or the way sounds faded in and out.

A hand touched her arm. She smiled at her aunt Janie, who had insisted on attending with her, because it was a short drive from home, and well, because Aunt Janie went nearly everywhere that Willow went.

"Didn't you hear me?" Janie asked.

"Of course I did."

"No, you didn't. I've asked you the same thing three times."

"I'm sorry, I'm just distracted." Willow slid her finger up the back of her ear. The hearing aid was at its maximum. And Janie was waiting for an answer that Willow didn't have.

"I said, I have a friend I want you to meet." Janie searched Willow's face, her growing concern evident in her eyes.

"Don't, Janie, please don't give me that look. It's the batteries, nothing more."

"Make an appointment with your doctor."

"Who's the friend?" Willow went back to the previous conversation. At that moment, even if it meant meeting a man, Willow wanted to avoid discussing the fact that she hadn't heard her aunt. Discussing it would only make her deteriorating hearing more real.

"My old neighbor, Clint Cameron, is here."

"Clint?" Not a stranger, but a forgotten crush. Willow remembered now, and she didn't want to remember.

She was too old for high-school crushes, and she had experienced too much heartache to go back to being that girl who dreamed of forever.

Her marriage to Brad Michaels had been a hard lesson in reality. Willow was still forgiving him and still letting go of her own forever-dreams that had ended five years ago, with divorce.

She was still forgetting, and still healing.

She was still finding faith, a faith that had been a whisper of something intangible for most of her life. Now it was real and sustaining. Somewhere along the road she had realized that she wasn't flawed, and she didn't have to be perfect.

Janie touched her arm again. "Are you with me?"

"I'm with you."

"It won't hurt, Willow."

"You think?"

Janie laughed, "It won't hurt, I promise."

"Of course it won't. I'm just amazed that I unloaded the bulls, fed them, and you found a friend."

"The Lord works…"

"In mysterious ways." Willow wanted to sigh. Instead she smiled for her aunt. "Okay, let me make sure my bulls have water, and I'll come find you."

"Good." Janie smiled a little too big. "He's parked on the other side of the pens."

Willow waited until Janie walked away and then started toward the pens that held her bulls. If she had any sense at all, she would hide and avoid meeting Clint Cameron for a second time. The first meeting had been a pretty big disaster.

The bulls milled around their pen, big animals with flies swarming their thick hides. They stomped in an effort to rid themselves of the flying pests, big hooves sloshing in the mud left behind after last night's rain.

Willow leaned against the metal gate, needing that moment to pull it together, to let go of fear. The water trough was full—taking her last option for avoiding Janie and her friend.

She had accomplished a lot in the last few years. She'd made it in a man's world, raising some of the best bucking bulls in the country and supplying stock for some of the biggest bull-riding events in the world.

She had survived Brad's rejection. His rejection

had hurt worse than the ones that came before him. She'd really thought that he meant their marriage vows.

He hadn't. He hadn't meant it when he repeated "in sickness and in health," or "till death do us part." He hadn't meant it when he said she was the only woman for him.

Willow watched her bulls for a few more minutes, and then she turned to go in search of her aunt and Clint Cameron.

She remembered the first time she'd met him, a cowboy in faded jeans, torn at the knees. She remembered a smile that had put her teenage dreams of forever into overdrive. She'd spent the next year wrapped in daydreams of a guy that she'd been afraid to talk to.

In search of Janie, she made her way through the crowd, greeting a few people who called out or waved. Bulls were being run through the gates of the nearest pens to the chutes where the riders would climb on for the ride of their lives. A few men were getting bull ropes ready for their rides.

She finally spotted her aunt. Janie stood at the edge of the crowd. Next to her was a man Willow didn't recognize. He looked nothing like the blurred memory of a gangly teen with faded jeans and a stained T-shirt. This man wore a bent-up cowboy hat with the faded imprint of a hoof. The strong angles of his jaw proved he was no longer a kid.

His Kevlar vest, worn to protect his torso from the

horns—or hooves—of an angry bull, was open, exposing a pale-blue paisley shirt. Tan leather chaps covered his jean-clad legs, brushing the tops of his boots. As Willow approached, he bent to catch something her aunt was saying.

Janie waved, motioning her forward. Willow waved back, reminding herself that she was stronger now than she'd ever been. But feeling strong when faced with a childhood dream wasn't as easy as she'd thought it would be. Especially when the dream was now a flesh-and-blood man with a wide smile and his arm wrapped protectively around her aunt.

Willow reached down deep and found strength, reminding herself that her new dream wasn't about happy-ever-after with a man. Her goals were now being achieved with a truck-load of bulls and success in the sport of bull riding.

But she wondered if he remembered her. Did he remember how she had said hello some sixteen years earlier, and then disappeared into Janie's house to watch from the window? He had spotted her there, waving when no one was watching. Even now the memory brought a flush of heat to her cheeks.

Willow took the last ten steps, joining her aunt and Clint Cameron. He took off his hat, revealing sandy blond hair that looked like it had been cut with electric clippers. Probably in front of a hotel mirror.

He should have used the clippers on his face. His five o'clock shadow was a day old, covering his sun-tanned cheeks and highlighting a mouth that turned in a slow, easy grin. Gray eyes, laugh lines crinkling at the corners, connected with hers.

On his off days he probably modeled for a cologne company with a typical western name—something like *Prairie Wind* or *Naughty Pine*. She smiled, trying hard not to look at the names of his sponsors, for fear she'd actually see *Naughty Pine* emblazoned on his sleeve or collar.

He wasn't a gangly teen anymore. And her heart still did that funny dance when he smiled at her. As a girl, not quite fourteen, she hadn't known what to do with that reaction. Now she carefully stomped it down, because she didn't need complications.

"Willow, this is my old neighbor, Clint Cameron."

He held out a hand and Willow let him take hers in a handshake that meant his fingers clasping around hers, holding tight for just a moment before releasing.

"Nice to meet you, Clint." Maybe he wouldn't remember her, the awkward kid who had stumbled through a greeting and then hurried back to the house.

He did, though. She could see it in his eyes. He smiled, revealing a tiny dimple in his left cheek that could have been a scar.

"Nice to meet you again, Willow."

"Clint's moving home. He's going to remodel his old farm house." Janie's eyes went liquid for a moment, and Willow knew what this meant to her aunt, to have someone back who had meant so much to her. "And he's made the points to ride in bigger events."

"Congratulations." Willow smiled, and then took a step back. "I'm sure we'll be seeing you around."

Janie caught her arm, stopping the perfectly planned escape. "I told Clint we might have some work for him to do. You know, I'm not getting any younger. It wouldn't hurt to have an extra pair of hands around the place."

"We can talk about that, Janie." Willow smiled at Clint Cameron. His gray eyes twinkled, and he saluted her with a tip of his hat as he put it back on his head, pushing it into place.

"If you don't have a lot for me to do, that's fine." He shrugged, like he really meant it. "I'm going to be working on our old farm down the road from you, getting it fit to live in."

"We'll work something out."

Clint Cameron smiled again, and Willow felt a twinge of regret, because she no longer believed in happy-ever-after with a cowboy.

Those dreams had faded a long time ago, victims of rejection and reality.

As Willow Michaels walked away, Clint drew in a deep breath and did his best not to whistle in surprise. He'd heard all about the tall stock contractor with the long, honey-blond hair and eyes the color of a clear spring sky.

Meeting her changed everything, though. He hadn't been prepared for a woman as cool and detached as a barn cat, the kind that didn't care if you paid attention to it or not.

He hadn't been prepared for the girl he'd met years ago, now a woman. What a woman.

"Don't let her scare you off, Clint. She's had a tough time of it, but she's coming around."

He smiled down at Janie. She'd been about the closest thing he'd ever had to a mother. His own mother had died when he was barely eleven and his sister was seven. He'd been left to raise Jenna by himself, and to deal with their drunken father.

Janie had been there to keep the pieces together.

She'd done the most important thing of all: she'd taught him to have faith. She'd also taught him to believe in himself. If it hadn't been for her he wouldn't have gone to college. He might have ended up just like his dad.

Janie had a new project. She was fixing her niece, Willow. Will for short, or so he'd heard. He couldn't imagine calling her Will.

"I should go. I'm one of the first riders up." He shifted away from Janie, but she caught hold of his arm.

"Think about what I asked you, Clint."

"Have you even told Willow that you want to move to Florida?"

Janie shook her head. "No, not yet. This business means so much to her. I've been putting off my decision because I was afraid Willow would give it up on my account. I don't want her to think she has to sell her bulls. If she had someone else she could comfortably rely on, the transition would be easier."

"I don't think she'd appreciate you trying to arrange her life this way. And I'm not going to push myself off on her, Janie. She's proven herself in this business, and I think she'll handle making this decision on her own."

He softened the words with a smile, because he didn't want to hurt Janie, the woman who had fixed a broken teenager, helping him to believe in himself. She wanted to do the same thing for her niece.

But Clint didn't plan on pushing his way into a life that had more Do Not Enter signs than a mine field.

Relationships weren't his strong suit. A long time ago he'd realized that he had a habit of choosing girls, and then women, who needed to be fixed in some way. Not that he thought Willow Michaels needed to be fixed. He just wasn't taking chances.

Not only that, but she was way out of his league. Another aspect in relationships that clearly didn't work.

He scanned the crowd and spotted Willow in a line for the hamburger stand that was a fundraiser for the National Future Farmers of America Organization. The aroma of grilled burgers drifted, and had lured a long line of people. Willow stood next to another stock contractor, her expression animated as they carried on a conversation.

He couldn't help but smile.

"You know, Janie, I have a feeling that Willow is a stronger person than you think."

"Of course she is, but she can't drive these bulls all over the country without some help."

"Seems to me that she can."

Janie smiled, her soft brown eyes twinkling. "Clint Cameron, if I didn't know better, I'd say you were trying to put me in my place."

"I'm only saying that I don't know your niece, but I have a feeling she can handle things." He fastened his Kevlar vest as he spoke. "If you want to move, Janie, you just need to tell her."

Janie laughed, "You should have come home more often. I've missed having someone around who wasn't afraid of me."

"I had a job."

"Working down there on those oil rigs in the Gulf. What kind of job is that for a country boy who wants to ride bulls and raise cows?"

"It paid the bills. It put money in the bank." Money meant for repairs on a farm that had gone downhill.

"Well, I know it was good honest work. I'm only saying that I missed you."

Clint leaned and kissed her powdery soft cheek. "I missed you, too."

"You go ride that bull. But be careful. We need you in one piece."

Clint laughed as he walked away. He laughed because Miss Janie had always had a knack for drama. It was a strange trait for a sensible woman.

As he threaded his way through the men standing near the chutes where the first few bulls were penned up and ready for their rides, he caught sight of Willow. She stood near a small group of people, her gaze concentrating on their faces as she read their lips. She nodded at something one of the men said and then she shifted her attention, focusing on Clint. Like she'd felt him staring. And for that moment, he couldn't look away.

He nearly ran into one of the event judges. The guy grabbed his arm and shot him a look.

"Sorry about that," Clint mumbled as he lifted his bull rope and continued moving through the crowd.

"You're up, Cameron." One of the men motioned him forward.

The MC in the announcer's stand gave the name of the next bull and followed that with Clint's name and a little information on his career. Of course they just *had* to mention that he was thirty-one, a late bloomer for bull riding.

He'd been at the sport for as long as he could remember. He just hadn't had the time to invest into making it a career. That didn't interest the crowd. They wanted to think about the old guy, the newcomer. Even in bull riding the fans wanted a Cinderella story.

Clint slid onto the back of a big old bull, one that he'd come up against before. Part Brahma and part Angus, the bull had a mean streak a mile wide.

A warm night in May didn't make the bull any nicer. The animal slid to his knees and then back up again, leaning to the left and pushing Clint's leg against the side of the chute.

One of the other riders, a guy named Mike, pulled the bull rope and handed it to Clint. Clint rubbed rosin up and down the rope and then wrapped it around his gloved riding hand. The bull lurched forward and someone grabbed the back of Clint's shirt, keeping his head from bashing into the metal gate in front of him. The animal shook its head and flung white foam across Clint's face.

Clint leaned forward, the heaving, fifteen-hundred-pound animal moving beneath him. Fear in the guise of adrenaline shot through his veins, pumping his heart into overdrive. The bull calmed down for a brief moment, and Clint nodded.

The gate opened, and the bull made a spinning jump out of the chute, knocking his back end against the corner and sending Clint headfirst toward the animal's horns. With his free arm in the air, whipping back for control, Clint moved himself back to center.

Eight seconds, and he felt every twist, every jump, every lurch. As the buzzer rang, Clint dived off for safety, not expecting the last-minute direction change that the bull added in for fun. Clint hit the ground, and the impact felt like hitting a truck. A loud pop echoed in his ears, and pain shot from his shoulder down his arm.

The bull turned and charged at him. He rolled away, but he couldn't escape the rampaging animal, its hot breath in Clint's face and the hammering of its hooves against solid-packed dirt.

That big old bull was face-to-face with him, pawing and twisting. Clint rolled away from the hooves and then felt a hard tug as someone jerked him backward, away from danger.

The bullfighter yelled at him to move. Clint did his best to oblige, but his left arm hung at his side, useless. The pop he'd heard when he hit the ground must have been his shoulder dislocating.

A blur of blue in front of him, and the bull changed direction to go after the bullfighter. Those guys were bodyguards and stuntmen, all in one package. Clint hurried to the side of the arena and the fence.

As he held on to the fence, watching the bullfighters play with the overzealous bull, he caught a flash of blond. He turned and saw Willow Michaels watching from the corner gate.

When he limped out of the arena, his eyes met hers for a split second and then she walked away. She wasn't the first princess to turn her back on him. She probably wouldn't be the last.

Telling himself it didn't matter didn't feel as good as it usually did. Fortunately he had the throbbing pain in his arm to keep his mind off the blow to his ego.

Medics were waiting for him as he walked out the gate. They offered help walking that he didn't need. He'd dislocated his shoulder before, so he knew the drill. He just didn't feel like talking about it.

"Want some help getting in?" One of the paramedics motioned inside the back of the vehicle.

"I'll just sit on the tailgate." He had no desire to climb, with or without help.

"Suit yourself."

He leaned back and just as he started to close his eyes, Janie was there. She wore that "mother hen" look that he remembered from his childhood.

It was a shame she'd never had kids of her own. But then he might have missed out on having her in his life.

"Is it dislocated?" She nearly pushed the paramedics aside.

"I imagine it is." He managed a smile that he hoped wasn't too much of a grimace.

"Do you need to go to the hospital?"

"I think the paramedics can manage."

Janie didn't look convinced. She was five-foot-nothing but a force to be reckoned with. Funny how she hadn't really aged.

Not like his dad. His dad was barely sixty-five, but already an old, old man. His liver was shot, and his mind was going. Janie would always have her wits about her.

"Don't let him sit there and suffer." She stepped back, and motioned the paramedics forward.

She had no idea about suffering. The pain he had felt just sitting there was nothing compared to that moment when they yanked his arm and pushed it back into its socket. Working through it meant a serious "cowboy up" moment. He took a few deep breaths that didn't really help.

"There, nothing to it." One paramedic smiled as he said the words.

"Yeah, nothing to it." Clint shrugged to loosen the

muscle, but the pain shot down his arm and across his back.

"It'll be sore, and I'm afraid there might be more damage than just the dislocation. Best get it checked out with the sports medicine team. Until then," he held out a sling, "pain meds, and you might want to get a ride home tonight."

A ride home? For the first time in a dozen years a "ride home" meant a ride to Grove, Oklahoma. And now it meant Willow Michaels living just down the road. He couldn't quite picture her as the "girl next door."

## Chapter Two

In the midnight-black of the truck, lit only with the red-and-orange glow from the dash, Willow nudged at the cowboy sleeping in the seat next to her. They'd driven the two hours from Tulsa and were getting close to the ranch. Janie hadn't helped. She had fallen asleep shortly after they'd taken off.

"Wake up." She nudged Clint again, careful to hit his ribs, not the arm held against his chest with a sling. "Do you have a key to get into this place?"

He stirred, brushed a hand through hair that wasn't long enough to get messy and then yawned. He blinked a few times and looked at her like he couldn't quite remember who she was.

"Willow Michaels, remember? We offered you a ride home?"

He nodded and then he shook his head. "I don't know."

She didn't hear the rest because he yawned and

covered his mouth. Moments like this were not easy for her, not in the dark cab of a truck, not with someone she didn't really know.

He said something else that she didn't catch. Willow sighed because it wasn't fair, and she didn't want to have this conversation with him.

This kind of insecurity belonged to a ten-year-old girl saying goodbye to her parents and wondering why they no longer wanted her with them. And always assuming that it was because her hearing loss embarrassed them.

He said something else that she didn't catch.

"Clint, you have to talk more clearly. I can't see you, and I don't know what you're saying."

There, it was said, and she'd survived. But it ached deep down, where her confidence should have been but wasn't.

He looked at her, his smile apologetic as he reached to turn on the overhead light. The dim glow undid her calm, because the look in his eyes touched something deep inside. Wow, she really wanted to believe in fairy tales.

Sorry.

And when he signed the word, his hand a fist circling over his chest, she didn't know how to react. But she recognized what she felt—unnerved and taken by surprise. When was the last time a cowboy had taken her by surprise?

She cleared her throat and nodded. And then she answered, because he was waiting.

"It isn't your fault. It's dark, and you didn't know."

How did he know sign language, and how did he know that it made hearing him so much easier? Even with hearing aids, being in the dark made understanding a muffled voice difficult—especially with the diesel engine of the truck.

"I know it isn't my fault, but I should have thought." He shifted in the seat, turning to face her as he spoke. "I'm sorry, I'm not quite awake."

"About the house?"

"I don't need a key to the house."

"Aunt Janie, you should wake up now." Willow downshifted as they drove through the small almost-town that they lived near. Grove was another fifteen miles farther down the road, but it was easier to say they were from Grove than to give the name of a town with no population and no dot on the map. Dawson, population 10, on a good day. The town boasted a feed store and, well, nothing else.

"Janie, wake up." Willow leaned to look at her aunt.

Janie snorted but then started to snore again. The vibration of Clint's laughter shook the seat. Willow shot him a look, and then she smiled. He had used sign language—that meant she had to give him a break.

She was still trying to wrap her mind around that fact. It had been a long time since someone had done something like that for her. Something unexpected.

"Where did you learn sign language?"

He shrugged. "I picked it up in college. I have a teaching degree, and I thought sign language would be a great second language. Everyone else was studying Spanish, French or German."

He signed as he spoke, and Willow nodded. She reached to shift again as the speed limit decreased.

"I'm rusty, so you'll have to excuse me if I say the wrong thing."

"You're fine." And the sooner she dropped him off at the little house surrounded by weeds and rusted-out trucks, the sooner she could get back to her world and to thoughts that were less confusing.

The driveway to his place was barely discernable, just a dirt path mixed in with weeds and one broken reflector to show where it was safe to turn. She slowed, not sure what to do. The trailer hooked to her truck jolted a little as the vehicle decelerated and the bulls shifted, restless for home.

"Don't pull in. You won't be able to turn the truck."

She agreed with him on that. She didn't have a desire to get stuck or to have a flat tire. Not with a load of homesick bulls in a stock trailer hooked to the back of her truck.

"But what are you going to do about tonight? Do you even have electricity?"

"I dropped off flashlights and a few other necessities this morning. Don't worry, I'll be fine." In the light of the cab he had stopped signing, but he spoke facing her.

The snoring from the far side of the cab had stopped. Aunt Janie sat up, yawning. "Clint, don't tell me you plan on staying here tonight?"

"There isn't that much night left, Janie. I'll be fine. Take Willow home, and get some rest. She's got to be tired after the day you two put in."

"You've had a long day, too." Willow pushed aside something that felt like anger, but maybe came from leftover feelings of inadequacy.

It had more to do with the past than with the present. It had to do with Brad telling their limo driver to take her home while he went into town, to a party that would have been too stressful for her to attend.

Alone. She'd always been at home alone. And she'd been sent away when she failed to meet expectations. The past, she reminded herself. It was all in the past and God had restored her life, showing her that she didn't belong in a corner alone.

She mattered to God. He had given her an inner peace and the ability to believe in herself.

"You're right about that." He stood in the open door, holding Janie's hand as she got back into the truck. "You two have a good night. See you tomorrow."

Tomorrow. When he would invade her life. Willow couldn't really thank him for that, not if he was going to be another person who found it easy to believe her hearing loss meant she couldn't take care of herself.

Clint woke up after a short few hours of sleep, stiff and sore, his arm throbbing against his chest. He rolled over on the sleeping bag and stared out the cobweb-covered window, so dirty that it might as well have had a curtain covering it. His savings account had seemed more than enough until he got a good look at this place.

Six months since his last visit home and two years since he'd been in this house. It looked like the dust had been there since then, or before. Not to mention his dad's old truck, tires flat and the frame rusting, growing weeds at the side of the house.

His dad had moved to a house in town two years earlier, and then to the nursing home. It hadn't been easy, putting him there, knowing he needed full-time care.

Clint's phone rang, and he reached for it, dragging it to his ear as he flipped it open. His sister said a soft hello.

"You sound bad. Do you look bad?" She laughed when he groaned an answer.

"Other than a dislocated shoulder, I had a great night."

"Sounds like fun. I'm sorry I missed it."

"Wait until you come down for a visit. Janie is still Janie. And her niece is living here."

"The one that used to visit in the summer?"

"The one and only."

"Is she still beautiful?" She was determined to see him married off.

"If you like tall, blond and gorgeous, she's okay." He rubbed his hand across his face, trying to rub the sleep away. "She isn't my type."

"Have you ever found your type?"

"Nope. I'm happily single."

"I don't think so, brother dear. I think you need a

woman to soften your rough edges. You need someone who will take care of you, the way you've taken care of everyone else."

"I don't have rough edges. So, what's up, Sis?"

He knew there was more to this call. He thought he might need to sit up, because the tone of her voice, even with the laughter, hinted at bad news. Holding the phone with his ear, he pushed himself up with his right hand and then slid back against the box of supplies he left here yesterday.

"What's up, Jen?"

A long pause and he thought he heard her sob. He didn't hear the boys, his twin nephews, in the background. His stomach tightened.

"Time to put our Family Action Plan into place. I'm going to Iraq."

Not that. He could have prepared himself for almost anything, but not the thought of his kid sister in Iraq. And the boys, just four years old, without a mom. He couldn't think about that, either. They had discussed it some. He had just convinced himself it wouldn't come to this—to her leaving and the boys in his care.

"Clint, I need for you to take the boys."

"You know I will. But there has to be someone better for them than me, an uncle who rides bulls for a living and who's camping in a house without electricity." For the moment.

"You're it. You're my only family, their only family. You knew this could happen."

"I want to make sure this is the best thing for them, that I'm the best thing."

"You were the best for me."

He closed his eyes, wishing he had been the best for her, and that he'd been able to give her more. He'd done his best. They both knew that.

"When?"

"I have to leave for Texas in five days. I've known for a while, but I guess I was hoping that something would happen and I wouldn't have to leave them." She sobbed into the phone. "Clint, they're my babies."

"I know, Jen. And you know I'll take care of them."

"If something happens…"

"We're not going to discuss that. But you know I love them and I'm going to take care of them until you get home."

She was crying, hundreds of miles away at a base in Missouri. She was crying, and he couldn't make it better. Sleeping under this roof, in this room, he remembered the other nights she had cried, when they had been kids, and he'd sneaked in to comfort her, to promise he'd make it better.

He had prayed, and she had doubted God even existed.

"I can't make this better, Jen."

"You do make it better." She sniffled, her tears obviously over. "Clint, the Army has been good for me, you know that. And I'm ready to go. I know that I have to go."

"But it won't be easy."

"It's easier knowing that you'll have Timmy and David."

"Do you want to bring them here, or should I come to you?"

A long pause, and he heard the sob she tried to swallow. "I want to see Dad before I go."

He looked out the dirt-covered window at the tree branch scraping against the glass, forced into movement by the wind. "Yes, you should see him. And it would probably be better for them if you got them settled here."

"I'll be down in two days," she whispered, and he knew she was crying. And he felt a lot like he might cry, too.

How was he going to let his little sister go to war, and how was he going to take care of two four-year-old boys? And then there was Willow, added by Janie to the list of people who needed his help.

Covered with dust and bits of hay, Willow walked to the door of the barn to see what the dog, Bell, was barking at. Of course it was Clint Cameron walking down the drive, a tall figure in faded jeans and a blue-gray T-shirt. A baseball cap shaded his face and his arm was still in a sling. She shook her head. Cowboys.

She brushed her hands through her hair and shook the hem of her shirt to rid herself of the hay that had dropped down her neck. Clint didn't spot her. As he walked up the steps to the house, Willow turned back into the barn.

She tossed a few more bales of hay into the back of her truck and cut the wires that held them together. A quick glance at the sky confirmed her suspicions that a spring storm was heading their way. The temperature had dropped ten degrees, dark clouds loomed on the horizon and the leaves of the trees had turned, exposing the underside. A sure sign of rain.

Before the rain hit, she needed to feed her animals. Cattle and horses were waiting and the bulls were bellowing from their pens because they knew it was breakfast time. She opened the feed-room door and stepped inside. The tabby cat that lived in the barn scooted inside and sniffed around in the corners of the room, looking for mice.

Willow grabbed a fifty-pound bag of grain off the pile and carried it out of the room. As she lifted, preparing to drop it into the back of the truck, Clint stepped through the open double doors of the barn and walked toward her.

She dropped the bag of grain into the back and returned to the feed room. When she stepped out with another bag, he was leaning against the side of her truck.

"Need some help?"

Willow tossed the second bag of grain. "I've got it. And I think it's probably better if you give your shoulder a couple of weeks to heal."

"Yeah, probably." He moved away from her truck. "Willow, I'm not trying to take over or anything. Janie told me you might need some help around here, and I'm a pretty good hand. If you don't need help…"

He tilted his head to one side, a soft look in eyes that were more the color of the ocean—gray with a hint of green—rather than just a shade of gray.

She shrugged. "A kid from down the road helps out sometimes. There are times when I can use more help."

"Hey, that's cool. I need to get work done on my own place, so I don't want full-time work right now." He moved away from her truck. "I wanted to see if you had some tools I could borrow."

"Tools."

He nodded. "To borrow."

"Yes, I know, I heard." She sighed, pushing down the insecurity his presence brought out in her. "Tell me what you need and I'll find them for you."

"It looks like rain, so I thought I'd pull a tarp over a section of the roof of my place. There are a couple of spots that look like they might leak."

"How are you going to climb a ladder?"

"I can handle it."

"I can give you a ride to your place." Willow pointed to a toolbox in the corner of the feed room. "See if I have what you need."

As he dug through the tools, she finished loading the grain. He stepped back out of the feed room and set the metal box in the back of her truck with a brown-paper bag of nails left over from one of her own repair jobs.

"You've done a lot with this place. When did you build this barn?" He leaned against the side of her truck, his baseball cap pushed back, giving her full view of his eyes. Eyes that flashed with a smile that for a moment put her at ease.

"I had the barn built two years ago. The fences—" white vinyl that always looked clean "—we put up last year."

"It looks good." He was smiling, and then he laughed a little. "Just seems like an odd choice."

"White vinyl fences?" She smiled, because she knew what he meant. Some men had a problem, a hang-up, with a woman raising bucking bulls.

"No, you, here, raising bulls. I seem to remember that you grew up in Europe."

That was part of the story. She didn't feel the need to tell him everything. She closed the door to the feed room and turned to face him.

"I did, other than a few summer visits to see Janie, but I love living in the country. And I love raising these bulls."

"I can help you feed before you run me over to my place."

"If you want, you can help." She walked to the driver's side of the truck. When she got in, he was opening the door on the passenger's side. "Did one of those guys drive your truck home this morning?"

"My neighbor, Jason Bradshaw's sister, drove it home."

She nodded, her gaze settling on his shoulder. "Do you need to see a doctor?"

"No, I know the drill. It'll be sore a few days, and then it won't."

She shifted into first gear and eased away from the barn. Her bulls were in the field behind the building. She had smaller pens for her "problem children" and a pen for calves that were being weaned. The cows that were expecting she kept in the main pasture with her horses.

Brad had done one thing for her in their divorce that she hadn't had in their marriage. He'd given her freedom in the form of a hefty divorce settlement. For the first time in her life she was her own person. Other than Janie's motherly advice, no one told her what to do. Not anymore. No one made decisions for her.

There was no one to walk out on her.

"I'm impressed with what you've done here, but I guess I still don't get it. You could have raised horses."

"I could have done something safe?" She smiled at the hint of red coloring his cheeks. "Years ago I went to a bull ride with Aunt Janie. I've been hooked ever since. It just seemed like the right choice."

It made her feel strong.

"It seems to fit you."

She smiled at the compliment.

"Thank you." She eased the truck through the gate of the first pen and stopped. "I'll get in the back of the truck and feed, if you can drive? Just ease down this lane next to the fence and stop at the feeders."

"I can do that."

As she slid out of the truck, he moved across the seat behind the wheel. She climbed into the back of the truck and used a pocketknife to slit the top of a bag of grain. As the truck slowed and pulled close to the feeder, she dumped the grain and the cows trotted forward, ready for breakfast.

The rain started to fall just as they were finishing. Willow jumped down from the back of the truck and climbed into the passenger side. Rain dripped from her hat and she rubbed her arms to chase away the chill. Clint reached for the heater and turned it up a few degrees.

"Wow, this is going to be bad." She looked up at the dark clouds rolling across the Oklahoma sky. "And you have a leaky roof."

"I do at that."

So softly spoken, she barely caught the words. For the past few months she'd been telling herself it was her imagination. But now she needed to face the truth. Words were fuzzy, and there were times that she couldn't hear a conversation on her cell phone, or even a person at her side.

Progressive hearing loss, the doctor had told them so many years ago. In the beginning it had been so mild, no one noticed, not really. Sometimes kids don't listen, that's how they had interpreted her behavior.

Progressive, but for years the change had been gradual, nearly unnoticeable. Now the changes to her hearing were very noticeable.

Why now?

She closed her eyes, and when she opened them, he was watching. Willow managed a smile and nodded in the direction of the house.

"We'll go in and have a cup of tea with Janie. Maybe the rain will stop."

"Sounds good." He pulled the truck to a stop in front of the long, log-sided ranch house.

Rain poured down, drenching them as they hurried up the steps to the covered front porch. Janie opened the door, handing them each a towel.

"Dry your hair."

Willow took off her hat and wiped her face and then ran the towel through her hair. "We were on our way to fix Clint's roof."

Thunder crashed and the rain shifted, blowing onto the porch. Janie opened the door and motioned them inside. With the rain hitting the metal roof of the porch, it was impossible to hear.

Inside the rain was muffled, and ceiling fans brushed cooler air through the room. Willow shivered again.

"Clint will have to stay in the foreman's house." Janie pointed for them to wipe their feet on the rug. "When it stops raining, Willow can take you over to get your stuff."

"I have a house, Janie."

"You can't live in that place. The roof leaks, the porch is falling in and it'll be weeks before the power company gets out to run new lines." Janie shot Willow a look, one that made her wish she could glance away and not hear what her aunt was about to say. "Tell him to stay, Willow. You need the help, and he can't live in that house."

Willow sat down on the old church pew Janie had

bought from an antique store. She kicked off her boots and slid them under the seat. Standing across from her, Clint held on to the door frame and pulled off his boots.

"The foreman's house is in good shape. Janie even keeps it clean. The furniture isn't the best…"

"I'm not worried about the furniture."

Janie smiled. "There, it's all settled."

"Right." Willow smiled, hoping that was a good enough answer. But it changed everything. It put Clint Cameron firmly in her life.

She followed her aunt into the kitchen, lured by the smell of coffee and something baking in the oven. Clint followed.

Janie continued to talk as she washed a few dishes. Willow poured herself a cup of coffee and listened, but she knew she was missing pieces of the conversation. The plan included Clint at the ranch in the foreman's house, and Willow letting him help with the bulls, and with the driving when they went out of town.

Clint, his stance casual as he leaned against the kitchen counter, shot Willow an apologetic smile. When Janie turned away for a brief moment, he signed that he was sorry. And she didn't know what to do with that gesture, that moment.

It wasn't easy, to smile, to let it go. After all of this time, building a new life, his presence made her feel vulnerable, weak.

Weak in a way that settled in her knees and made her want to tell him secrets on a summer night. She

sighed and walked out of the room, away from gray
eyes that distracted and away from the memories of
long-forgotten dreams.

Clint set his tea glass on the table. He didn't want
to follow Willow Michaels out the door, but he
couldn't let her walk away. This was the pattern of his
life. There had been the cheerleader in high school
who had been hiding abuse with a smile, and he'd
found her crying. The girl down the road who had
been planning to run away from home when she found
out she was pregnant.

He followed Willow to the hall where she was putting
her boots back on. She looked up, mascara smeared
from the rain and her hair hanging over her shoulders,
still damp. She smiled as he sat down next to her.

"I'm not trying to hijack your life." He signed as
he whispered, because he didn't want Janie to
overhear and misinterpret.

"I know." She pulled on her second boot and sat
back. "I just need for you to know that I'm not inca-
pable of doing this by myself. I don't mind you living
here, or even helping out."

"I know that." He glanced at his watch. "I have to
visit my dad. But I need to talk to you about something."

"Follow me out to the barn. I need to check on a
young bull that I have there. He has a cut on his leg.
I think he got into some old barbed wire."

He nodded and reached for his boots. As he put
them on, Willow walked into the kitchen. He could

hear her telling Janie that she was going to check on a bull, and then she'd drive him back to his place to get his truck.

A few minutes later they walked out the door. The sun was peeking out from behind clouds, and the rain had slowed to a mist. The breeze caught the sweet scent of wild roses, and it felt good to be home.

The dog, Bell, ran from the barn and circled them, stopping right in front of Willow before rolling over to have her belly rubbed. Willow leaned to pet the animal and then she turned her attention back to him.

"So, what did you need to talk about?"

"My nephews."

"You have nephews?"

"Twins, they're four years old." He stopped, rubbing a shoulder that hurt like crazy, thanks to the rain and sleeping on the floor. "My sister is being sent to Iraq."

"Clint, I'm sorry." Her voice was soft, her accent something indiscernible with only a hint of Oklahoma.

"She wants me to take them while she's gone."

Her gaze drifted away from him, and she nodded. Shadows flickered in her eyes and he wondered what put them there? Him? The boys? Something from her own life? What made a woman like her give up everything and move to Oklahoma?

Maybe she'd found what she was looking for here, with Janie, and cattle? He could understand that. He'd lived in cities, small towns, and here, on land that had been in his family for nearly one hundred years. He preferred this place to any other.

"It won't be easy," she spoke in quiet tones, "for any of you."

"No, it won't. But I wanted to make sure it's okay with you. Now there will be me *and* two little boys underfoot."

She smiled. "Of course it's okay. We'll do whatever we can to help you out."

"I appreciate that." He headed for the barn, following her, and still wondering what had put the shadows in her eyes.

But he didn't have time to think about it, to worry about it. He had to think about his dad, and now about Jenna and the boys.

## Chapter Three

Clint walked through the halls of the nursing home, not at all soothed by the green walls that were probably meant to keep people calm. Even with his dad here and in bad health, Clint still felt like the kid that never knew what to expect. That came from years of conditioning. His dad had been the kind of drunk that could be happy and boisterous one minute, and angry enough to hurt someone the next.

As much as he wanted to convince himself that the past didn't matter, it did. And forgiving mattered, too. Forgiving was something a person decided to do.

He'd made his decision a long time ago. He'd made his decision on his knees at the front of the little country church he'd gone to as a kid. He'd found faith, grabbing hold of promises that made sense when nothing else had.

But being back here brought back a ton of feelings, memories of being the kid in school who never had a new pair of jeans or a pair of shoes without holes.

He'd always been the kid whose parents didn't show up for programs or games.

He reminded himself that he wasn't that kid. Not now. He had moved on. He had finished college. He had worked his way up in the sport of bull riding. He hadn't made a lot of money, but at least he had something to show for his life.

His attention returned to the halls of the nursing home, sweet old people sitting in chairs next to the doors to their rooms, hoping that someone would stop and say hello. A few of them spoke, remembering him from a long time ago, or from his visit last week.

His own father sometimes remembered him, and sometimes didn't.

"Well, there you are." Today was a day his dad remembered.

"Dad, how are you?" Clint grabbed the handles of the wheelchair and pushed his dad into the room.

"I didn't say I wanted to come in here."

"I don't want to stand in the hall." Clint sat on the bed with the quilted bedspread and raggedy stuffed elephant that one of Jenna's boys had left for their granddad, even though their granddad rarely acknowledged their presence.

"So, did you find a job?" his dad quizzed as his trembling hand reached for a glass of water.

Clint picked up the glass and filled it from the pitcher on the table. He eased it into his dad's hand. It was full and a little sloshed out. Clint wiped it up with a napkin and sat back down on the bed.

"I have a job. I'm a bull rider. And I'm going to work for Janie."

"That old woman? Why would you work for her?"

Clint glanced out the small window that let in dim afternoon light shadowed by the dark clouds of another storm. He had to shrug off his dad's comments, the same comments he'd always made about Janie.

There were questions Clint would like to ask now. Did his dad really dislike Janie, or was he just embarrassed that her money had put food on their table and clothes on their backs? He breathed deep and let go of the anger.

Too many years had gone by to remind his father of that time, and to hurt him with the truth that would have sounded like accusations. He stood and walked to the window. Behind him his dad coughed.

"I could use a drink."

Clint shrugged but didn't turn away from the window, and the view of someone's hayfield. A tractor sat abandoned in the middle of the field, half the hay cut and the other half still standing. Something must have broken on the tractor. Not that it mattered. But for a moment he needed to think about something other than the past, and his dad still needing a drink, even with his liver failing.

"Where's your sister? Is she home from school yet?"

His dad had slipped into the past, too.

Clint turned, shaking his head as he sat down on the bed. It was easy to forgive a man who was broken. The surprising thing was that he even felt compassion.

"Dad, Jenna is in Missouri. She's going to Iraq."

"Why would she do that?"

"She's in the Army." He took the water glass from his dad and set it on the table. "Dad, do you remember? Jenna is twenty-seven. She has two little boys."

"She shouldn't have had them without a father. She should have married that boy."

"He didn't ask." Clint had to fight back a remaining shard of anger over that situation. The ramblings of an old man he could overlook. The past could be forgiven. His sister being hurt, that was something he still had to work on.

"What's your sister going to do with those boys?"

"I'm going to take care of them."

His dad laughed. "You? How are you going to take care of two little boys? Do you even have a job, other than working for Janie?"

"I'm helping her niece with the bucking bulls she raises."

His dad's eyes widened at that and then narrowed as he smiled. "Are you in love with her? I imagine she's way out of your league."

How could one conversation reduce him from grown man to a sixteen-year-old kid teaching the judge's daughter to ride the horse she'd gotten for her birthday? *Way out of your league* must have been the statement that took him back.

"No, Dad, I'm not in love with Willow Michaels. She needs help, and I need a job."

"I need to take a nap, and you need to find out why Jenna didn't come home on the bus. She hasn't even fed the chickens."

"Okay, Dad, I'll go check on her." Clint stood, towering over his dad's frail body. Before he left, he leaned and hugged the old man who had hurt them all so much.

Forgiving had been taken care of. Forgetting was getting easier.

Now he had to go home, to the foreman's house and get it ready for the boys. He tried not to think about that house not being his, or about the home he'd grown up in not being a fit place for two boys.

As he climbed into his truck, he tried, but couldn't quite block the thoughts returning, thoughts of Jenna leaving the boys. He tried not to think about her being gone for a year, and what could happen in that time. And he tried not to think about living a dirt trail away from Willow Michaels—*who was way out of his league.*

Six in the morning, Willow was barely awake, and as she glanced out the kitchen window she saw two little boys run across the lawn, heading toward the barn. Two days ago Clint had asked her if she would be okay with the twins living on the farm, and now they were here. She hadn't thought about them being here so soon.

The bigger problem now was that the boys were running for the pen that held her big old bull, Dolly. She set her glass of water down on the counter and hurried for the front door. Janie, sitting in the living room, looked up from her Bible, brows raised over the top of her reading glasses.

"Is there a fire?"

"No, but there are two little boys heading for Dolly's pen."

Dolly was her first bull. At bull-riding events they called him Skewer, because it was easier on a cowboy's ego to get thrown from a "Skewer" than a "Dolly." Gentle or not, she didn't want the two little boys in that pen.

As she ran across the lawn, she glanced toward the foreman's house. A small sedan was parked out front, the same one she'd seen easing down the driveway yesterday. No one was outside. The boys, silvery-blond hair glinting in the sun, weren't slowing down. They obviously had a plan they wanted to carry out before the adults realized they'd escaped.

Willow hurried after them, rocks biting into her bare feet. If she didn't catch them in time… She shook off that thought, that image. She would get to them in time.

"Don't go in there," she shouted, cupping her mouth with her hands, hoping the words would carry and not get swept away on the early morning breeze.

The boys stopped, turning sun-browned faces in her direction, sweet faces with matching Kool-Aid mustaches. They were armed with paper airplanes and toy soldiers.

Willow's heart ka-thumped against her ribs. Fear and remnants of loss got tangled inside her. She had to stop, take a deep breath, and move forward. The way she'd been moving forward for the last five years, one step at a time. Rebuilding her life.

The boys were watching her, waiting.

She reached them and they stared up at her. Their eyes were wide and gray, familiar because up close they looked a lot like Clint Cameron.

Their gazes shot past her. She turned as Clint and a young woman walked out of the foreman's house. The two, brother and sister, paused on the front porch and then headed in her direction.

"Uh-oh," one of the boys mumbled and his thumb went to his mouth.

"Don't suck your thumb," the other shoved him with his elbow, pushing him hard enough to knock the slighter-built of the two off-balance.

"You two do know that it isn't safe to go in the barn or around the bulls, right?" Willow knelt in front of them, her heart catching.

They nodded. The smaller boy tried to hide the thumb in his mouth by covering it with his other hand. Their twin gazes slid from her face to something behind her. *Clint?*

She stood and turned, ready to greet him and his sister. The little boys scurried to the side of their mother, their hands reaching for hers.

"Clint." Willow didn't know what else to say. She didn't know that she wanted to say more.

"Willow, these two rowdy guys are my nephews. This is my sister, Jenna."

Jenna, brown hair streaked with blond highlights and petite frame clothed in shorts and a T-shirt, held out her hand. "Nice to meet you. And I'm really thankful to you for giving Clint a place to keep the boys."

"You're welcome, Jenna. We're glad we can do it."

Willow squatted to put herself at eye level with the two little boys, matching bookends with identical looks of sadness and fear. Their mother was leaving. Willow fought the urge to pull them close, to promise that everything would be okay.

She thought about her own fears, her own longings. It all paled in comparison to what this family was going through.

"My name is Willow. What are your names?"

"Timmy," the bigger of the two pushed at his brother again, "and this is Davie."

"David," the boy mumbled, looking down at the ground.

Insecure? She understood insecure, and how it felt to not know where she was supposed to be, or what she should do.

Janie had joined them, and she was hugging Clint's sister, holding her tight for a long minute while the boys held tight to their mother. When Janie turned back around, tears shimmered on the surface of her eyes.

"Jenna doesn't have a thing to worry about, does she, Willow? We'll be here to help Clint with the boys until she can make it home."

Willow smiled at the boys again. Just little boys, and they were going to have to say goodbye to their mother. She'd been ten when her parents sent her away, forcing her to leave their home in Europe and attend a special school in the States.

She knew how hard it was to let go of what was familiar. She also knew that Jenna's heart had to be breaking, because nothing hurt a mother worse than letting go of a child.

"Of course we'll help." Willow ignored Clint, because she couldn't look into his eyes. She couldn't acknowledge, not even to herself, how hard this was going to be.

Janie smiled, her brown eyes soft. Janie knew.

Time to escape. Willow ruffled the blond hair of the smaller boy, and he looked up at her, gray eyes seeking something, probably answers. She didn't have any. She could pray, but a child didn't want to hear that, because he wouldn't understand what God could do. At his age, the little guy just wanted his mom to stay with him.

"I need to get my shoes and get some work done." Willow smiled at Jenna, who seemed unsure and probably needed reassurance. "Don't worry about the boys, or Clint. We have plenty of room here."

"Thank you." And then Jenna hugged her.

"I'm sure we'll see you before you go." Willow pulled away, from Jenna and the situation. "Boys, remember, stay out of the pens."

Clint started to follow her, but she stopped him. "I can handle this. You spend time with your sister."

"You're sure?"

Positive. What she needed was time alone, to think about how her life had just changed. What she didn't need was Clint Cameron invading space she had carved out for herself. And what she couldn't do was look into his gray eyes, eyes like those of his nephews, but seeing so much more.

A few hours later Jenna drove down the road, and Clint could only pray that God would keep her safe. Janie had the boys, feeding them cookies and drying their tears. He was going in search of Willow to see if she needed help with anything, and knowing she would probably say that she didn't. She had a way of handling things.

Country music blared from the office at the end of the barn. Clint peeked around the corner of the office door. She wasn't there. An empty soda can sat on her desk, along with the wrapper from a chocolate bar, more than one. He smiled, thinking of her sitting there with music blaring, eating chocolate. What did that do for women?

So much for the calm, cool facade that she'd fooled them with in the bull-riding world. He now knew her weakness. Ms. Calm-Cool-and-Collected ate chocolate and didn't like to share her personal space.

That knowledge didn't help him out a bit. He was definitely in her personal space, and with no way out.

He found her in the arena, standing on a platform above a bull and strapping a training dummy to his back while she talked into the headset of her cell phone. Her brows drew together, and her lips tightened into a frown.

Obviously bad news.

He approached from her side, making sure she knew he was heading her way. She nodded and turned away, maybe to open the chute for the bull, maybe to avoid him. The gate on the chute opened, and the bull turned to face out, encouraged by the woman above his chute. A teenager, slight, and quick on his feet, stood in the arena, keeping the bull in a spin.

"Looks good. How old?" Clint leaned against the post next to Willow.

Her hand slid up her ear.

"I'm sorry?" She smiled.

"The bull looks good. How old is he?"

"He's two. I'm not sure if he's going to make it. He doesn't like to buck."

"Do you need my help? I can open the gate, strap on the dummy?"

A pointed look at his shoulder. "I don't think you should."

"Got it." Help not needed. He had to find his place here. He had to apologize. "I'm sorry about the boys this morning."

"They were being boys, Clint. They're fine." She leaned against the rail of the scaffolding next to the chute where the next bull was waiting. Her expression softened, because it was about two little boys. "How are they, though?"

"They're okay." He remembered their tears when

Jenna left, and his own. They were all fine. And scared. "At least they're here with me. We'll get through."

"If I can help…"

"You have."

Another one of those looks he didn't understand, and shadows in her blue eyes that could probably convince a man that she needed to be held. But he knew better than to step into her life. There was a world of difference between them.

She was designer clothes and gourmet meals. He was fast food and the clearance rack at Wal-Mart. And he liked his life. For the moment he looked a lot happier with this discount life than she looked with her top-drawer existence.

She turned away from him to watch the bull come out of the chute and then she shook her head. "Brian, run him through the gate, and we'll get him something to eat. Bring Wooly in next."

"Willow, if I'm going to live here, I really want to help out."

"Have you been to the doctor yet?" She shot a pointed look at his shoulder, his arm still in a sling.

"Not yet. It's an injury I've had before, and I know what to do."

"So, you'll be ready to ride bulls at the next event. Or are you going to call and let them know that you'll be a no-show."

"You know I can't do that and stay on tour."

"Then go to the doctor. If you can't afford…"

"I can afford it."

He sure didn't need insults and charity.

"I'm sorry." She picked up the training dummy that Brian had tossed onto the platform and leaned to put it on the new bull. "We'll work together. I don't know specific jobs to give you. I know each day what I need to get done. And if something unexpected comes up, I fit it into my schedule. I guess we start with you helping us with feeding time."

Her phone rang and she smiled an apology and stepped away from him. At least now he knew how he stood, at the ranch, and in her world. He was one of the unexpected things she was fitting into her life.

"I'm sorry, I can't hear you." Willow walked away, knowing that Clint wasn't the kind of guy to purposely listen in on a conversation, but knowing that if he heard, he would have questions.

The caller on the other end apologized for the bad connection. She closed her eyes, wishing it really was a problem with the phone. But the bad connection had nothing to do with cell service.

She glanced in Clint's direction and saw him talking to Brian. Distracted, she had to gather her thoughts and listen to the caller as he told her something about a bull she had for sale.

"Sir, could you call me back on my home phone? Or perhaps e-mail." She held her breath, praying he'd say yes and wondering if God heard such selfish prayers.

It wasn't selfish, not really. Because God did understand her fear. She'd talked to Him about it quite a bit lately.

"I'll e-mail." The caller came through clearly for a moment, and she thanked him. She needed a break, a real break, the kind that meant things going smoothly for a few days.

Just a few days, time to gather herself and figure out her next move. She turned, facing Brian and Clint with a smile that felt strong. But eye contact with Clint wasn't helping her feel strong. It was the way his lips quirked in a half grin and lines crinkled around his eyes.

He had a toothpaste-commercial smile that could make a girl dream of moonlit nights and roses. She no longer had those dreams.

"Where are the boys?" Neutral ground that felt safe, safer than holding his gaze.

"Janie is fixing them grilled cheese for supper, after she's already filled them up with cookies." He leaned to hold the dummy for Brian. "We're going to the chili supper and carnival at church tonight."

"Yes, she told me. That's a good way to distract the boys. The next few days are going to be hard for them."

"She told me you're not going."

She wondered if he understood what it meant to invade someone's personal space. It wasn't always done physically. Sometimes it was done emotionally, with nosy questions and interference. Maybe he didn't care?

"No, I'm not going."

"Because…"

She stepped away from him. "Because I don't like chili."

Because she didn't like crowded places with too many conversations, explanations for people who talked in quiet tones, and curious glances from those who saw the hearing aids.

She loved bull riding, where people respected her and curiosity didn't matter, because she had proven herself. She loved her non-hearing friends in Tulsa, because with them she could be herself.

He didn't appear to be giving up. He had stepped closer and wore a persuasive half grin. She remembered him smiling like that when she'd been thirteen and he'd only been a year or so older. She had dreamed of that smile for a long, long time, wondering what it would be like to fall in love with a cowboy.

She shook off the old memories and listened to what he was saying now. Now, sixteen years and several rejections later, her heart had been broken so many times it was held together with duct tape.

"Everyone likes chili. Or at least they like it when they know there will be dozens of desserts, and the money is going to help the church youth group."

Willow liked arguing less than she liked chili. Worse than that, she disliked the feeling that someone was trying to make plans for her. "I'm not going, Clint. I'll give you a check for the youth group."

"Willow, I wasn't trying…"

She sighed, because she knew that he wasn't trying, that he hadn't intended to take over. "I know you weren't. Have a good time tonight. Make sure you guys close up and turn off the lights when you're done in here."

Clint reached for her arm, and she knew he wanted to say more. He didn't. Instead he smiled and let his hand drop to his side, like he understood.

As she walked across the drive to the house she saw the boys through the window. They were so young, and so brave. Their mother was brave.

The warm smell of grilled cheese and fresh coffee greeted her as she walked through the door of the house. She kicked off her boots and headed for the kitchen, stockinged feet on hardwood.

The boys looked up from cups of tomato soup, red liquid dripping from their chins. She smiled, but she wanted to hug them tight. The little one, David, not Davie, gave her a tremulous smile that threaded its way into her heart. The bigger of the two, Timmy, just frowned.

"I heard that the two of you had cookies. Were they good?" Willow kneeled next to the table, putting herself at eye level with the two children.

They nodded and both took another bite of their sandwiches, dripping cheese as they pulled the bread away. Grilled cheese and tomato soup, Aunt Janie's cure for everything, including broken hearts.

"Want something…" Janie's words faded out as she moved away.

Willow turned, shooting her aunt a questioning gaze. The words had blended with the radio and the dishwasher's low rumble.

"I'm sorry, Willow. Do you want to eat, or are you going with us?"

"I'll eat with the boys." Willow smiled at the two and stood up, her legs protesting her squatting next to the table.

"The boys are going with us." Janie smiled. "But they don't like chili."

"I don't blame them."

Janie frowned. "It isn't chili you're avoiding, it's people."

"And lectures."

Janie wiped wet hands on a kitchen towel, her frown growing. "Willow, are you okay?"

"Of course I am."

The house vibrated with footsteps, heavy steps. Willow turned as Clint walked into the room, his wide smile directed at the boys.

Janie handed her a bowl, and Willow turned toward the table. Clint had taken a seat with the boys. He had a glass of iced tea and a cookie.

"You have a cow that's about to have a calf," he said after taking a drink of his tea.

"I know. I've been checking on her every few hours."

"Is this her first calf?"

"Second."

"She's young."

Willow exhaled and pretended she didn't have an

answer for that. He set his glass down and she looked up, knowing he wasn't going to let it go.

"Yes, she's young. The first time she got into the wrong pen." She wouldn't go further, not with two little boys at the table.

"Maybe I should stay home, in case she gets down on you. You might have to pull the calf."

Like she didn't know that. She gave him a pointed look and lifted a spoon of soup to her mouth. After taking a bite she set the spoon down.

"I can handle it, Clint. I know how to pull a calf. I know how to take care of my cows."

"I was just offering."

"If I can't handle it, I have a good vet." She took in a breath and smiled. "You need to take the boys to the carnival at church. I can handle this."

He raised his hand and smiled. "Got it."

Timmy laughed and David looked worried.

"Guys, don't ever argue with a woman who has her mind made up." Clint picked up a napkin and wiped grilled cheese crumbs off David's chin.

Willow smiled, because how could she not? And when she looked up, he winked. Just like that, he undid everything.

## Chapter Four

Clint threw another plastic ring around another soda bottle and took the two-liter cola that the girl handed him. The low rumble of a diesel engine caught his attention. He turned and watched as Willow pulled into the parking lot of the church. She backed the red extended cab into a space and cut the engine.

And he smiled. Unexpected. She was obviously a woman who always did the unexpected. He liked that about her. And he liked the fact that she was here, and she had made it pretty clear that this was the last place she wanted to be.

But she was getting out of her truck, and she was smiling. At him. That smile made him want to win big stuffed bears for her and carry cotton candy. It made him want to…

Rescue a woman who didn't want or need to be rescued.

"Uncle Clint, isn't that Miss Willow?" Timmy tugged on the sling and Clint grimaced.

"Yeah, buddy, that's her. You boys stay with Janie, and I'll bring her over here."

Because he wanted just a few minutes alone with her. A smile shouldn't do that to a guy. It shouldn't make him want to take her off by the creek, alone, for a walk in the dim glow of early evening. A smile shouldn't do that to a man, but it did.

That smile made him want to forget that she was a princess and he had nothing to offer but a crumbled old farm and a lot of dreams.

She stopped at the edge of the parking lot and waited for him. She was tall and gorgeous, in jeans and a peasant top, her hair in a ponytail.

"Imagine seeing you here." He grinned and hoped that she would smile again. She did.

"I decided that if the boys could do this, so could I." She glanced past him to the boys. "They're really brave."

"They are." He started to offer his hand and reconsidered. "Stick with me, it won't be that bad."

Had he just said that? From the amused look on her face, he knew he had. He pushed his hat down on his head a little and laughed.

"Stick with you, huh?"

"Something like that. I'll even hold your hand."

"I'm a big girl. I won't get lost." She looked past him again, and she didn't take his hand. "The boys are heading this way. I'm really here for them, not you."

"Ouch, that hurts a guy's ego."

She turned to face him, and he knew she hadn't heard. He repeated and she smiled.

"I think your ego will be fine."

"You're probably right." And on the chance that she would hold his hand, he held it out again, palm up. She took it, her fingers grasping his and he felt like he might be her lifeline.

When they reached the twins, she let go of his hand and reached for the boys. They moved to her, and for a minute it made him really believe they might be okay. He hadn't expected that she'd be the one to make him feel that way.

"What is there to do around here?" she asked David, always the quiet twin, always seeking assurance.

"I like the pony ride and…"

"The big bouncing castle." Timmy grabbed her hand.

"Pony ride first." She put an arm around each and smiled at her aunt. Watching her with the boys, Clint wanted to be four again and small enough for ponies and the moonwalk.

"What about me?" he asked, hurrying to catch up. Willow glanced back at him.

"You're too big for the moonwalk."

"I'm not too big."

"Uh-huh." Timmy had hold of Willow's hand. "And you promised us cotton candy."

"Cotton candy, of course. And I have a pile of prizes I need to put in the truck."

Willow stopped, still holding on to the boys. "I'll take them on the pony ride."

"Sounds good." He didn't really want to walk away. He wanted to stay with her, with the boys, because she was easy to be around.

But he had been dismissed, and the boys got to hang out with Willow. He felt a little cheated as he walked off with nothing but stuffed animals and bottles of cola.

Willow lifted David onto the back of a brown-and-white spotted pony. He leaned toward her, his gray eyes big. "I'm afraid of horses."

She smiled and wanted to tell him that it was okay, that fear sometimes pushed a person to be strong. He was too little to understand. He only knew that he was afraid.

"I'll stay next to you."

He nodded and then the horse moved a jolting step forward. Little hands grabbed the saddle horn and his mouth tightened into a serious line. Willow patted his arm and winked.

"Pretend he's one of those purple horses in front of the grocery store. They bounce, but they don't move." She kept hold of his arm. "He can't go anywhere but in a circle. And if he tries, I'll grab you."

"Promise." His voice was soft and she read his lips.

"Promise." She wouldn't let him go.

She searched the crowd for Janie and Clint. Janie had found a group of friends, and they were all sitting under a canopy. She spotted Clint walking in their direction, three sticks of pink cotton candy in his hands.

Even without the cotton candy, he stood out in the

crowd. He was a cowboy in faded jeans and a dark-blue polo. His hat shaded his face but didn't hide the smile that she somehow imagined was just for her.

For a moment she was like David on his pony, not afraid, just enjoying the ride.

But what about tomorrow? What about reality?

How long could she go on, pretending everything was fine? How long could she convince herself that she wasn't afraid? Who would catch her?

She knew the answer to that. She would catch herself.

"Could we ride again?" Timmy yelled from his horse.

"One more time." She pulled tickets from her pocket and handed them to John, a neighbor who was donating his time and his ponies for the youth group to raise money for a mission trip.

He took the tickets and said something to each of the boys about being cowboys like their uncle.

Clint walked along the outside of the portable fence that circled the ponies. "Cotton candy?"

He held one out to her. The pony turned his head and nipped, wanting the sugar more than Willow wanted it. David laughed, a real laugh. He hunched, and his shoulders shook. Willow laughed, too, and then Timmy was laughing. The pony didn't care; she wanted the sugar and the bar that kept her going in her circle clanked as she stretched out her neck.

The boys continued to laugh, and Willow wiped tears from her eyes. When she looked up, Clint was watching, his dimpled grin now familiar.

The ride ended. She helped David down. Timmy hopped to the ground, a little cowboy in his jeans, boots and a plaid shirt. Janie and Clint were waiting for them at the gate. The boys took their cotton candy.

"I'd like to take the boys in to have their pictures taken," Janie announced. "Sandy is in there with her camera."

"Sounds like a great idea." Clint held out the last cotton candy and Willow took it, surprised that it was for her. "Do you mind if I take Willow for a buggy ride?"

Willow swallowed a sticky-sweet bite of cotton candy, remembering why she liked it so much, and also why she hadn't eaten it in years. "Clint, I have to leave. I wanted to spend a little time with the boys, but I have to get home to that cow."

Under the wide brim of his white cowboy hat, his brows arched in question. He didn't believe her. Of course he didn't. For a moment, she didn't believe herself. She had come down here for the boys, and then for other reasons. Maybe because she wanted to walk with a cowboy and eat cotton candy?

"I really do have to go. She's close to having that calf, and I don't want to lose either of them."

"Of course." He smiled and she remembered that his smile was the reason she'd jumped in her truck and driven down to the church.

She averted her eyes and glanced down at the boys, each holding cotton candy that was nearly gone. "You two have fun."

They nodded but took another bite of spun sugar. They wouldn't sleep for a week. She laughed a little and turned to face Janie and Clint.

"I'll see you all later." She made her escape. It was definitely an escape, she realized that. She was running from someone who made her feel too much.

And she had more reasons for running than he could possibly know.

Clint woke up at daybreak, the sun just peeking over the flat, Oklahoma horizon. He looked in at the boys, still sound asleep. They'd stayed late at the church, where the boys had played games, throwing rings around soda bottles and darts at balloons. They now had a cabinet full of root beer, and a bag of cheap toys and stuffed animals, all prizes from the games they'd played after Willow left.

At least the cow had been more than just an excuse. The proof was the spindly-legged calf standing next to her momma in the corral next to the barn.

Sometimes he wondered if she gave anyone a chance to really know her. Or was it just about him? He could still remember her peeking through the curtains all those years ago, hiding. Embarrassed?

He put on a pot of coffee and then went to wake the boys. David was already stirring, his eyes blinking open a few times and then catching with Clint's.

How did he do this? How could he be a parent when he didn't have any experience, other than having been an older brother? Doubts hung out in the pit of his stomach when he thought about it.

Clint kneeled next to the twin bed and smiled at the little boy, a child with his sister's dimples. Clint closed his eyes, praying for them to get through the next year, and praying for Jenna to stay safe.

She had to come home to the boys. They all needed her. He included. David leaned on one scraped elbow, his eyes sad. Clint mussed the kid's hair and tried to pretend they were all okay, and that he knew how to be the parent they needed.

"How about cereal for breakfast?" Clint asked as David sat up, rubbing sleep-filled eyes.

"We like pancakes," Timmy's groggy voice said from the other bed.

Clint turned, smiling at the other twin. "I don't think I have stuff for pancakes, Timmy."

"Aunt Janie does. She said so. Last night she said," and he cleared his throat to make the point, "'you boys come over in the morning, and I'll whip you up some homemade pancakes.'"

Four years old and a mimic. Clint laughed at the fair imitation.

"Okay, we'll go to Janie's for pancakes." He stood, stiff from squatting, and from too many times landing on a hard-packed dirt arena. "Get dressed, okay?"

"I don't want pancakes." David covered his head with the blanket. "I want my mom."

The words were muffled, but the emotion wasn't, or the slight sob that followed.

Clint stood at the door, his heart squeezing. "I know, buddy. But she'll be home as soon as she can get here."

In a year. One year of her children's lives, lost. One year of missing milestones. One year of him worrying, and praying she'd be safe.

He smiled at Timmy. "Help your brother get ready."

One year of life on hold for all of them.

A short time later, he walked out of Janie's and across the road to the barn. The boys were eating pancakes, and Janie was hugging them, pretending the tears in her eyes were from dust.

He walked through the large double doors at the front of the barn and was greeted by silence. Light poured out from the open door of Willow's office.

He stopped at the entrance. She stood at the window, looking out over the field. Her forehead rested on the glass of the window and her hands were shoved into the front pockets of her jeans.

After a few minutes, he said her name. She didn't turn, didn't even start. There was no indication that she'd noticed his arrival.

So how did he make his presence known, and keep from scaring her? He stepped up into the room and reached for her, but then pulled back. When she turned, she saw him there. She jumped a little and then exhaled.

"How long have you been here?" Her voice was husky, soft.

"A few minutes. I said your name."

She looked away. He noticed then that the hearing aids she normally wore weren't in sight. That was the reason for the silence, for the lack of music, and why she hadn't heard.

WILLOW, ARE YOU OKAY? He signed the words, stepping to block her from walking away.

She smiled. "I'm fine."

She sat down on the edge of her desk. "Are you okay?"

And that's how she changed it, making it about him, not her. It wasn't just deflection on her part. He could see in her eyes that she cared, that she wanted to know that he was okay. He was. It was the boys he wasn't so sure about.

"I'm fine."

"I don't think so."

HOW DO THEY LIVE FOR A YEAR WITHOUT THEIR MOM? He sat down next to her, signing the words. "Will there come a time when it doesn't hurt so much, when they don't cry because they miss her?"

"I don't know. She's their mom. I can't imagine them not missing her all the time."

Her voice broke and she brushed away a few tears, and he didn't know what to do. He couldn't fix them all. He was barely holding it together for his nephews, barely making life okay for his dad. He knew that they had to be his priority.

He had a bad habit of trying to take care of people, maybe because he'd been taking care of people his whole life.

Willow didn't want or need that from him. He had to remember that, and not get confused about what he was feeling for a woman who was a strange mixture of strength and vulnerability.

The boys. He shook his head. "I can't get David to eat."

"He's heartsick. Maybe ice cream? It's good for fixing a broken heart."

The low rumble of a truck pulling up out front interrupted his thoughts and stopped him from asking about her broken heart. ARE YOU EXPECTING COMPANY? he signed.

She glanced out the window and groaned. "No, not really."

"Looks like someone is here bright and early. Do you know who it is?" He spoke as he signed because he knew she read lips.

"Not a clue."

She ran a hand through long, blond hair. Tall and slim, she looked strong. In faded jeans and a long-sleeved shirt tucked in, she looked like every other cowgirl that he knew.

And then again, she looked a lot like someone trying to pretend.

"It's probably the man interested in that gray bull. He e-mailed." She admitted as she rummaged through papers on her desk, "I don't remember his name."

"He called yesterday?"

"I asked him to e-mail." She turned off the coffee pot on the desk. "Can you bring the bull up?"

"Do you need for me to talk to him?"

She bit down on her bottom lip and he hated that he had asked. But when she nodded, he no longer regretted. Sometimes accepting help made a person stronger. He wanted to tell her that, but she was walking away, and he couldn't say anything.

## Chapter Five

Willow walked out of the house, ready to face the man with the truck, and whatever questions he had for her. Janie had smiled as she left, but she'd been too busy with Timmy and David to ask questions.

At the door to the barn, she paused, giving herself a minute to regain her strength and to feel composed. The shadowy interior of the barn, with the smell of hay and animals blending together, did that for her. She loved hiding here, and praying here.

She loved Oklahoma and its wide openness. Growing up in Frankfurt, Germany, where her father had worked for the government, she had been surrounded by buildings, concrete and the smell of exhaust. Cities were exciting and had an energy all their own.

But living here gave Willow energy. This was her home, and it had always felt like it was where she belonged.

Here she could be the person she wanted to be, not the person others expected her to be. This place wasn't about black-tie dinners, pearls and putting on a smile for society.

At the end of the barn she saw Clint and the owner of the truck. Their stances were casual, but the movement of their hands, the way they faced one another, warned of something less than casual.

Willow approached cautiously, trying to hear their conversation, but the words were lost. Clint turned in her direction, his eyes relayed a warning she didn't get.

"Hello, I'm Willow Michaels." She held her hand out to the man who wasn't a rancher, not in his dark slacks and white button-down shirt.

"Ms. Michaels, I'm with the *Midwest Informer.* We're doing a feature on bulls used in bull riding. We're interested in a woman's point of view."

"I'm not sure…" She shot a look in Clint's direction. His lips had narrowed, and he gave a short shake of his head.

"The article is going to run whether you talk to us or not. We just wanted to give you a fair opportunity to talk about your bulls, and the abuse these animals suffer."

"Abuse?" She glanced again at Clint. His fingers signed for her to be careful.

And the reporter caught the gesture. She saw the light spark in his eyes and he smiled. "Ms. Michaels, you could be the feature of our article. A woman who raises bucking bulls. A disabled woman."

"I'm *not* disabled. And I'm not a feature, Mr...."

"James Duncan."

"Mr. Duncan, my bulls are not abused. My bulls receive excellent care, the best food and a home where they are prized for their abilities. I have nearly twenty animals that are actively used in bull riding, some in the top arenas, and some in smaller rodeos. Each month they work approximately ten minutes, ten minutes total, and yet they receive the best care. How can that be cruel?"

"They're forced to buck."

"No, they're not forced. If I have a bull that doesn't buck, then I sell him, because bulls either buck or they don't. And my bulls are protected from abuse." She ground out the words, no longer being careful. "The bull-riding community protects their animals, even at the events."

Her hands were shaking, and she knew that her voice had reached a higher octave. The man in front of her continued to smile, and out of the corner of her eye she saw Clint straighten from his relaxed pose, leaning against the barn.

Willow shook her head at him, not wanting him to intervene. He backed up, but he remained tense, like a guard dog about to do damage, and her heart reacted. She nearly smiled at the reporter.

"Mr. Duncan, I believe this interview is over. If you really want the truth, and not a sensationalized spin on my sport, then attend an event with us. Watch how my bulls are treated, and then write the article."

"That's a nice offer, Ms. Michaels, but I have my story."

He walked away, his steps light, as if what he had done didn't matter, as if he was happy with the way things had gone. And Willow was shaking, unable to stop because it did matter. It mattered when someone took away your strength or made you feel like less than a whole person.

She closed her eyes and took a deep breath. Strong arms pulled her close. She stiffened, but he didn't let go. And she didn't want to pull free. She wanted to melt into his embrace, and for just a minute, let herself be protected.

He bent and his cheek, rough and unshaved, brushed hers. His scent, mountain air and pine, teased her senses as his hands rubbed her arms and then slipped down to hold her hands.

"You were amazing."

No, amazing was how it felt to be held by someone who thought she had been strong, when she had really felt like walking away.

Slowly, regrettably, she backed out of his arms. "Now what happens? What story does he think he has that is better than the story of my bulls?"

"The story of you. The story of bulls. Or maybe of us."

"Us?"

He smiled, those gray eyes twinkling with amusement that she didn't get. "Us, because he thought there was an us."

"There is no us. There is no story. He's going to target a sport that I love, and my personal life. And there's nothing I can do about it, or about the rumors that will fly once that magazine comes out."

"No, Willow, there's nothing you can do about it." He shook his head. "I have work to do."

He walked away. A cowboy in faded jeans, scuffed boots, and calloused hands that had held her close. His expression as he turned from her had reflected his own pain, and something in his eyes she hadn't understood.

Willow walked into her office and closed the door. She yanked off her hearing aids and threw them in the box, because there were days when it didn't pay to hear.

And days when she feared she would lose her hearing completely.

She sat down in the leather office chair that swallowed her, wrapping around her, but feeling nothing like the arms of a cowboy.

Cowboys didn't understand how weakness felt, or fear. Maybe that wasn't fair. Clint had watched his sister leave for Iraq, leaving behind two little boys. He understood fear.

She bowed her head because God understood her fear. He understood forsaken. She whispered the words of Jesus on the cross, "My God, My God, why hast thou forsaken me."

Forsaken was how she had felt when her parents put her on a plane to Chicago. She had been ten years old, and frightened, but they had decided she needed to attend a private school for hearing-impaired children.

Forsaken was how she felt when her husband told her she couldn't be the wife he needed. He had ended it by telling her he needed a wife that would help his career. A wife who liked to socialize. A wife who didn't embarrass him.

He had picked her best friend to replace her.

Forsaken. But not. Even when she had felt alone, pushed aside, and rejected, God had been there, a prayer away. God hadn't forgotten her. He had a plan. Maybe not her plan, but His plan. And maybe it wouldn't be easy, but she had to convince herself there would be moments of beauty that would make all the pain worth it.

She reached into the box and withdrew the hearing aids, her life since age ten. It had started with meningitis she'd caught as a preschooler, and slowly progressed to severe hearing loss.

And now, now the slow progression was increasing. She slipped the pieces of plastic behind her ears and found the number of her doctor in Tulsa. The way to deal with fear was to confront it, head on.

When she walked out of the barn a short time later she had an appointment with her doctor. His nurse had told her that it was probably nothing.

Laughter carried across the lawn, soft and fluttery. Willow glanced in the direction of the driveway in front of the house. Clint was helping the boys into the truck. They were "three-of-a-kind," and that brought a smile she hadn't felt five minutes ago.

Little David turned and waved his tiny, sun-browned hand. His smile was timid and sweet. Timmy's wave was big, and his smile consumed his face. Sunlight glinted from their silvery-blond hair, and she knew that someday they would be carbon copies of their uncle.

Their uncle, Clint. He turned, a grimace on his face as he tried to smile with Timmy tugging on his left arm, still held to his side in a sling. Two weeks, the doctor had told him. Maybe longer. Not good news for a guy that made his living on the back of a bull.

She walked in their direction, drawn by the boys. She wanted to hug them. She wanted to promise them that their mother would come home. She wanted to apologize to Clint, but she didn't know what to say.

"Where are you three off to?" She smiled at the boys.

"We've gotta get in some kind of school." Timmy answered as he always did, mimicking the last adult to give him information.

She laughed, knowing that his words were an echo of something Clint had said to them. He had mentioned to her that the twins needed to enroll now for kindergarten in the fall.

"That sounds like fun." Her gaze lingered on David, because the look on his face told her he didn't agree that it would be fun.

"It will be fun." Clint chucked David under the chin, smiling at the child. "And after we enroll, we're going to get ice cream. Want to go with us?"

Willow hadn't expected that. She hadn't expected to be included, and hadn't thought she would want to say yes. The boys were watching her with twin gazes that said they wanted her to go. She looked up, connecting with Clint, and not sure if he really felt the same as the boys.

But the boys wanted her to go. And David needed to eat. She smiled at the twins.

"I could probably use your help." Clint shrugged the shoulder that was still healing. "Sometimes they're hard to hold on to."

Did he really need her help? Maybe not as much as she needed to spend time with Timmy and David, eating ice cream and laughing over silly jokes that children told.

"I'd love to go. Let me tell Janie."

"She isn't here. Her bridge group is meeting."

"Okay, then let me get my purse. If you need me to drive, it might help if I have my license."

"I can drive."

No more arguments or excuses. Willow climbed into the passenger seat of the truck. The boys climbed into the backseat. And then Clint was in the seat next to her, and she looked away. It was easier to glance in the backseat and smile at the boys, both jabbering about ice cream and school, childhood things that were easy and light.

Clint had watched Willow's smile disappear. He had seen the tears shimmering in her eyes. There could have been several reasons. The boys, maybe, or the reporter. Possibly the call he'd overheard her make. He hadn't listened to the entire conversation. He knew she'd called a doctor's office.

Seeing that soft shimmer of tears, and knowing her fear, helped him to push aside his anger with her, or whatever he had felt when she pulled away from him, saying things that made him think that she had her own thoughts about being out of his league. She didn't want rumors spread about the two of them.

"My aunt isn't really meeting with her bridge group." She smiled now. He took his attention off the road for just a second, long enough to see that she'd pulled herself together.

"Really?" He didn't want to get in the middle of this mess.

"She wants to move to Florida with her friends." Willow fiddled with a ring on her right hand. "She thinks I don't know. But a friend of hers was excited about the plan and let it slip."

"Willow, she doesn't want to hurt you."

"And I don't want to hurt her by keeping her here."

He wanted to ignore this side of her that cared about the happiness of others. He had already learned too much about Willow Michaels. He had learned that she was easy to like, and easy to care about. And he had a dad in a nursing home, and two boys to raise for the next year. He didn't need more complications.

She could be that and more.

"I'll miss her, Clint. But she isn't hurting me by doing what she has always wanted to do. When I was a teenager, she talked about retiring to Florida someday. She wants to go with friends. She wants to learn to play golf, and figure out what shuffleboard is all about."

"Does anyone really understand shuffleboard?"

"Someone must."

The day had started with a reporter ambushing her, and now they were talking about shuffleboard. She was a survivor. They had that in common.

"She's afraid you'll sell the bulls if she leaves."

He glanced away from the road, to see how she took that news. She was smiling.

"She's always looking out for me. When my parents shipped me off to Chicago, Janie met me at the airport. They didn't ask her to. She found out what they'd done, and she showed up without telling them. She didn't want a little girl to get off the plane alone, in a strange city, to be met by strangers."

"She bought our Christmas presents and put us through college." Clint smiled at the memory. "She didn't believe in storing up, for herself, 'treasure on earth, when there were little treasures down the road, needing so much.'"

"I will miss her if she goes." She was looking out the truck window. "But I won't sell the bulls. I'll figure out a way to make it work."

"Tell her that."

"I'll tell her." A short pause, and then she laughed. "That's why she wants you working on the ranch.

She's making sure I have someone to help me. I was afraid it was all about matchmaking."

"She's always trying to protect the people she cares about." But he had sort of thought it might be about matchmaking, too.

They drove toward Grove and past the house that Clint still planned to remodel. Soon. Clint's mind switched in that direction, and away from Willow, thinking about that house and what needed to be done. He thought about the cattle he wanted to raise on a farm that had been neglected for more years than he could count.

And then his thoughts returned to a part of their conversation that he had heard, but hadn't really thought about.

"Your parents sent you to the States alone? Why?"

She shrugged. "They had a busy schedule, school was starting. That summer they realized how bad my hearing was. I hadn't really noticed. Or maybe I had adjusted without realizing. As it got worse, I paid more attention to lips when people spoke, and I asked a lot of questions. But that summer my hearing got progressively worse."

The information poured out of her, surprising him. She was so matter-of-fact, so accepting. But he was imagining how it changed a person's life, to be unable to hear conversations, or to be left out of what was going on.

"But they sent you across the world, alone. That couldn't have been easy."

She shrugged as if it didn't matter, but he wondered if that was the truth. "Who has a perfect story, Clint? Not you, not me. Some have stories that are a little sweeter, with less pain. But almost everyone has a story. My parents love me, but they were busy with their careers. And frankly, I was a little embarrassing. I was a clunky kid with thick glasses, hearing aids and a penchant for hiding in corners."

"You were a clunky kid?"

"Tall, scrawny, and clunky."

She had more stories, he knew that. What had sent her running to Oklahoma and Aunt Janie? What kept her hiding in that corner and pushing people out of her life? Did it all go back to a little girl who thought she'd embarrassed her parents?

But she was right, everyone had a story. And he wouldn't push for hers. His story sat in the back seat of his truck, two little boys that needed him to focus on their lives, and their well-being. And he had a history of poor choices in the romance department that made him more than a little gun-shy.

As if she understood, Willow glanced over her shoulder, her smile real, and not meant for him. "You know what, guys? I think we should eat pizza before we have ice cream."

It was that easy for her to shift the conversation away from her, to make it about two little boys. He thought she'd had a lifetime of experience, deflecting attention from herself. She knew how to build walls.

He had built a few himself.

\* \* \*

Willow walked through the door that Clint held open for her and the boys. A wall of cold air greeted them: someone wasn't afraid to turn their air conditioner on before June. Willow shivered and the boys reached for her hands, one on either side.

She smiled at the hostess who mumbled something about seating them. A hand waved from across the restaurant. A farmer that had sold her a few cows. She nodded a greeting and then he noticed Clint.

"Great." Clint spoke close to her ear. "Here we go again."

"What?" Willow pulled out a chair at the table the hostess had led them to.

Before Clint could answer, the farmer, Dale Gordon, stood next to their table. He was a big guy, with striped overalls and a wide smile.

"Clint Cameron. I'd heard you were back in town. Don't tell me you're going to try and make something of that old farm."

"Sure am, Dale."

"Might as well sell it to me."

Now Willow understood. She pretended to help the two boys with their napkins as she listened to bits and pieces of conversation.

"I'm not going to sell something that's been in my family for over a hundred years, Dale."

"It was in my family first."

"Your granddaddy lost it in a poker game. Tough luck, but I'm not selling."

Dale laughed. "You've always been hardheaded."

"Sure have and so have you. I think we're cousins, at least six or seven removed."

"Something like that." Dale patted Clint on the back. "Let me know if you change your mind about the old place."

"Will do, Dale."

Willow smiled up at the waitress who had arrived to take their order. She was a cute girl with blond hair in a ponytail and pale blue eyes that sparkled with sunshine when she smiled at the boys.

"Can I take your order?"

Clint looked at Willow, waiting for her to order. Now would be the time to tell him she really didn't like pizza. She smiled and ordered a salad. Clint ordered a large pepperoni pizza.

"Has he always wanted that land?" Willow turned her coffee cup over for the waitress to fill it.

"For as long as I can remember. There were a few times I was afraid my dad would sell. He always sobered up and came to his senses."

She tried to picture Clint as a kid, holding his family together, the same way he was holding it together now.

"It couldn't have been easy."

His brows arched at that. "What couldn't have been?"

"Your dad."

"It wasn't all bad."

She waited for him to tell her more. But he didn't

share. Instead he moved aside their drinks and the napkin holder as the waitress arrived with their pizza. The boys lifted their plates for a slice, and for the first time in a long time, Willow was tempted by pizza. The crust was soft, and cheese dripped.

Clint laughed. "You can have a slice. Surely you're not on a diet."

She shook her head. "Nothing like that. I'm not much of a pizza person."

Both boys were staring, eyes wide. She felt like she'd just announced something scandalous. Clint laughed again.

"Have a slice, Willow."

Pizza, a day with Clint and the boys, and her heart tripping all over itself. Willow didn't know how much more she could handle.

"Okay, one slice." She took the plate with the pizza. Clint handed her a fork.

"You'll like it better if you just pick it up and eat it. But I have a feeling you're a knife-and-fork girl."

She didn't take the fork. "Don't make assumptions, Clint Cameron."

The pizza was hot, but she picked it up and took a bite. And she wasn't sorry that she had. She smiled at the boys as she pulled the slice away, cheese stringing along behind it.

"Okay, I admit it, pizza is good."

Clint put another slice on her plate and moved her salad aside. "Some things grow on a person."

Yes, some things did.

They were finishing lunch when Clint stood and pulled his phone out of the pocket of his jeans. Willow moved David's cup away from the edge of the table and shot a glance in the direction of the man walking away from them, the phone to his ear and his conversation lost to her.

"What kind of ice cream would you all like when we get to the ice cream parlor?" Willow smiled at Timmy, who licked sauce off his fingers and then reached for his soda. She handed him a napkin.

"I like bubble-gum-flavored." Timmy blew bubbles into his soda with his straw and spoke out of one corner of his mouth.

Willow couldn't have heard correctly. "Bubble gum?"

He nodded, "Ice cream."

It sounded disgusting. David didn't answer. His gaze held hers and she saw the tears form. "Oh, sweetie, what's wrong?"

"I like chocolate, and my mom puts stuff on it," he whispered, and his thumb went to his mouth. A look from Timmy, and he pulled it back.

Willow pulled him close and wanted to hold him forever, because she understood how it felt to lose something important. And she couldn't begin to know how a four-year-old could cope with that loss. Even if it was only temporary. He was a baby who needed his mommy to tuck him in, to tell him stories and sing to him.

Willow had always wanted to be someone's mommy. How did she tell a child that God understood, and that time really did heal? How could she promise him that God would bring his mom home safe?

David's sun-browned arms wrapped around her neck. A hand fell on her shoulder, and she pulled back. Clint stood next to her, his concerned gaze on her, and then on his nephew.

"That was the nursing home. They're having problems with my dad. I need to see if I can help them calm him down. Or give permission for them to take him to the hospital."

"Do you want me to stay with the boys? I could take them home."

He shook his head and his gaze lingered on Timmy first and then David. He was carrying the weight of the world on broad shoulders, but were they broad enough? His sister gone, his dad sick, and two boys who needed him.

How did he manage to take care of everyone, and himself?

"You could drop us off at the ice cream parlor," she suggested, hoping to make it easier for him, hoping he would see that she could handle two boys and ice cream.

He shook his head again at first, but then he smiled. "Okay, I'll drop you off. This shouldn't take long. And if it does, I'll text you."

Text, not call. She smiled. "Okay, it's a plan."

When she walked through the doors of the ice cream parlor with two little boys, each holding a hand, she felt a funny leap in her heart. For a short time, she could fill this role in their life. She could be the soft touch.

It was easy, dealing with them, loving them. They were safe.

Clint's dad had dementia. They'd explained it to him before, about small strokes and alcohol. But he didn't always grasp the reality of it until days like today, when his dad was angry at the world. He had thrown apple cake at a nurse's aide, made rude comments to one of the other residents and then fought with his nurse.

It didn't feel good, having to send him to the hospital. And now, it was hard to smile as he walked into the ice cream parlor. But he did smile.

He smiled because it was easy when he saw the boys scraping the bottoms of their bowls, and Willow licking around the edges of a cone.

David had finally eaten enough to make Clint feel like the kid might survive. The boy had even eaten a couple of slices of pizza.

"Hey, how did it go?" Willow asked, after a bite of cone.

"Good. He's fine." Okay, not fine. But Clint could take care of this on his own. He was used to taking care of his family.

He looked at the boys and realized just how much Willow and Janie had helped since Jenna left. With his arm still in a sling, and sore from the exercises the doctor had given him, keeping up with two boys was a chore.

Willow smiled and pointed to the seat next to hers.

"Thanks." He sat down, aware that she was six inches away and smelled like springtime.

"Want ice cream?" she offered, taking another bite of hers.

"No, I'm full from pizza." He patted his gut. "Got to stay in shape."

She laughed. "Oh, of course. I forgot."

"What, you don't think we take our sport seriously?"

"I know you do. I also know enough about bull riding to know you aren't sitting on the back of a bull for another couple of weeks."

"I think I have something to say about that."

"I think Dr. G does, too. She'll be back, and you'll be in big trouble."

"Well, I can't stay off tour for long."

Her smile faded. "I know."

"Thank you for doing this with the boys."

"I'm the one who's thankful. I've had a great afternoon."

Clint glanced at his watch. "I hate to ruin it. We should probably head home."

Home. He ran the word through his mind again. It had been easy, saying it like that. His home was really a run-down farm a half mile from hers. But her farm had become his home.

And she looked pretty uncomfortable with that.

## Chapter Six

Clint ran the bull into the chute, glad for the roof of Willow's indoor arena. The rain had started yesterday, after they got home from having ice cream, and it didn't look like it would let up any time soon. He really needed to practice before the next event. He needed to know that his shoulder would stand up to the pressure of riding.

Clint climbed on the back of the bull, remembering the first time he'd ridden one, and how that experience had made him feel. He'd loved the sport from the beginning—the challenge, the friendships, and even then, working out frustrations with his dad.

The bull, young and inexperienced, went to his knees in the chute. Clint nudged, hoping to convince the animal to stand. Brian, the kid who helped Willow part-time, reached through the gate and gave the bull a push.

"He ain't comin' out, Clint." The kid, sixteen and already missing a tooth from a bad bull wreck, grinned.

"Go ahead and open the gate." Clint leaned, tentatively preparing to lift his left arm, his free arm. It ached, but nothing he couldn't handle. He had to grit his teeth and get through it.

The gate opened, the bull stayed on his knees. Brian took his hat off and shook it at the animal. Like a bottle rocket, the bull exploded out of the gate, taking them both by surprise. Clint hunched, his shoulder protesting the sudden movement.

"Keep your chin tucked." The feminine voice carried, combining with the rush, the pounding of his heart and Brian whooping at the side of the arena. "Watch your free arm. He'll switch and spin left if he thinks he can't get you off to the right."

He heard, and listened. She knew the sport, and she knew what it took to stay on her bulls. But he had to think fast on a ride that could last seconds.

No buzzer. He finally took the leap, hoping to land on his feet, not his shoulder. He tripped as he went down and held his breath for contact with the ground. When he landed, he rolled, and the bull ran off. Good bull, giving a guy a break.

He stood, stiff, and afraid to test his shoulder. It hurt. That was all he needed to know at the moment. But he could move his arm. That was a plus.

"I don't know why you guys do it." Willow shook her head as she approached, picking her way across the arena in high heels that made her taller than ever, nearly as tall as he was.

He was tall for a bull rider. He liked that she didn't

have to look up to him. He liked that he could hug her and she'd be at eye level.

He wanted to hug her. But he smelled like bull, and she had walls. He didn't want to confuse the two possibilities—attraction, or just his stubborn need to protect. He didn't know which fit his feelings for her, and didn't want to analyze. And she was dressed to go out. He let his gaze slide over the black pants and black-and-white top with sheer, gauzy black sleeves. She smelled like something expensive and floral.

She cleared her throat. "Clint, should you be riding?"

"I needed some practice if I'm going to make that next event." He reminded her of the event she'd already questioned him about. "I can't afford to lose my sponsors."

"You can't afford a serious injury to your shoulder."

"I'm used to dealing with it, Willow. I know what I can take and what I can't." He glanced back at Brian. "Go ahead and put him up for the night."

"It was a good ride." Willow spoke, but she looked off toward the gate, not at him.

"Thanks. Where are you going?" None of his business, and he should have kept it that way.

"Tulsa. I'm meeting friends. I won't be home until tomorrow. Maybe late."

"What do I need to do around here?"

"If you can feed. And keep an eye on Janie."

He laughed at that. "Janie doesn't want a keeper any more than you do. The two of you are more alike than you realize."

"We know how to take care of ourselves, Janie and me."

She smiled, and his mouth went dry. He almost gave in to the urge to hug her, to hold her tight. He wanted to taste lips that smelled like strawberry lip gloss and bury his face in hair that smelled like citrus.

And those thoughts should have been enough to convince him that he was losing control, and forgetting his priorities. Two little boys, a sister in Iraq, and a dad slowly drifting away from reality.

His reality. No time for relationships, and no time for pursuing a woman that didn't want to be pursued.

"Well then, I guess I'll go." She took a step back, and he moved with her.

She looked vulnerable, and a little lost. He couldn't let her leave like that, no matter what his convictions, or hers. And he didn't plan on confusing his need to fix with love.

"Willow, are you okay?"

"Of course I am." She glanced away, and he wasn't convinced.

He touched her cheek to turn her, and her eyes closed. Before she could move away, he leaned, not pulling her to him but keeping his fingers on her cheek. He kissed the strawberry gloss, and she kissed him back.

When she stepped away, he saw regret. He hadn't wanted to make her regret. He didn't want to regret either. But maybe she was right. It was the wrong time, the wrong place.

She had walls that he didn't have time to climb or break down.

"See you in a couple of days." She touched his lips, wiping away the gloss. "We shouldn't do that again."

He didn't agree, but then again, he did.

The restaurant was dark and the conversation at the table was quiet, hands moving, sometimes words, and with the curious stares of people around them. Willow watched the lips of a friend, but her mind wasn't on conversation or friendship.

She was thinking about Clint, and the kiss. She was thinking about regret. She was thinking about tomorrow.

WHERE ARE YOU, WILLOW? Angel signed. Angel had been profoundly deaf since birth and didn't like to speak orally in public.

Willow smiled when Angel nudged her. "I'm sorry, I have a lot on my mind."

THE DOCTOR'S APPOINTMENT? Angel signed.

"And the man my aunt hired to help me."

IS HE CUTE?

"He's cute. He's likes to take care of people."

The waiter approached with plates of food. Willow waited until they were served before continuing. She sprinkled salt on her vegetables and passed the shaker to Angel.

CUTE *AND* SENSITIVE, Angel signed and shuddered. THAT'S BAD.

"I'm not saying it's bad."

Your ex-husband hurt you, Will, but that doesn't mean another guy would.

"I'm not going to let him, because I'm not looking for a relationship. I have a life now, the life I want."

Your life isn't reality, a life with no one telling you what to do. What's that all about? Angel's eyes sparkled with humor.

"It's safe."

Angel took a bite of pasta and spoke as she chewed, her hands signing with passion. "Safe" isn't living. "Safe" is a cocoon that shuts the world out.

Big words from Angel, who lived in the deaf culture, her world of choice. Willow lifted her brows, the only response needed to bring a smile from her friend. And then Angel signed, I'm dating someone.

"Hearing?"

Yes, hearing. Angel flushed a light pink. And he loves me.

"Where did you meet?"

You're not going to believe it.

"Try me."

Angel smiled. At the grocery store. My cart hit his, and he accused me of doing it on purpose.

Willow laughed. "Did you?"

She couldn't imagine her shy friend doing anything to draw attention to herself, but the pink in Angel's cheeks flushed a deeper shade.

"You didn't!" And then everyone was staring, people at their table, and at other tables.

Do you have to announce it to the world?

Angel reached for her glass of water and smiled at the curious friends, all waiting for an explanation.

I'M SORRY, Willow signed, and then explained to the others that she was happy for Angel, she had a new man in her life.

THE FIRST MAN IN MY LIFE. Angel's pink cheeks remained flushed. I'M TWENTY-SEVEN, AND FOR THE FIRST TIME IN MY LIFE, I THINK I MIGHT BE IN LOVE.

"I'm happy for you."

Angel shook her head. NO, YOU'RE WORRIED. YOU THINK HE'LL HURT ME. THE WAY BRAD HURT YOU. YOU THINK HE WON'T BE ABLE TO ACCEPT MY DEAFNESS.

"That isn't what I think." But didn't she feel that way? Hadn't she always believed her parents had sent her away out of embarrassment and Brad had divorced her for the same reason?

There had been other relationships. She didn't want to go down that path tonight, thinking about past hurts.

YES, YOU DO, WILLOW. YOU THINK HE'LL REJECT ME. Angel smiled to soften the words. BUT HE LOVES ME. AND WHEN SOMEONE LOVES YOU, THEY ACCEPT EVERY-THING ABOUT YOU. HE'S EVEN LEARNING SIGN LANGUAGE.

"You're right, and I'm sorry."

WHERE'S YOUR TRUST?

"Trust?" Willow thought maybe she'd heard wrong, in the shadowy light of the restaurant, maybe Angel had signed something other than the word "trust."

TRUST GOD. YOU NEVER KNOW WHAT HE CAN DO IF YOU OPEN YOURSELF UP.

"You're right, Angel. And I'm so glad you've found someone."

Willow hugged her friend and let the conversation end, because Angel deserved to be happy, and not all relationships ended in pain.

The words of the doctor the next day undid any feelings of strength she had imagined the previous night with Angel and her other friends. Sitting alone in his office, just a nurse for company, Willow listened as he explained that her hearing might continue to decline. To what degree, he couldn't be sure until the test results came in, but he wanted her to be prepared.

Prepared for profound hearing loss. A hearing loss that would make her hearing aids virtually useless.

For weeks she'd convinced herself that it wasn't happening. It was just her imagination. Now she had to face reality. If she couldn't hear, how would she manage at bull riding events? How would she keep her business going?

The doctor apologized, and then he handed her the card of a psychologist, because she might want to talk to someone. She numbly took the card and shoved it into her purse.

*My God, my God, why hast thou forsaken me?* Tears burned her eyes as she walked out of his office and down the hall, but she wouldn't let them fall. She wouldn't cry. Not yet. She would process this information and deal with it.

She would survive.

She would do more than survive. God hadn't brought her this far to forsake her. She hadn't started this new life to give it up. And there was a chance that the test results would come back and show that this was temporary. Or that the progression wouldn't continue.

She took a deep breath and tucked her purse under her arm, feeling stronger for having convinced herself to have faith. Sometimes it took a little convincing when things looked dark.

She saw him in the lobby, a figure in faded jeans and a polo, leaning against the wall near the water fountain. He was wearing his tired-looking straw hat, and a toothpick stuck out of the corner of his mouth. He straightened as she approached, his smile quick and sure. She hadn't been forsaken.

God had sent a friend.

And she really needed a friend. He held her gaze as she walked toward him. She remembered her regret yesterday, when he'd kissed her. She remembered the confusion she'd seen in his eyes.

But he was here now. That had to mean something.

How many times in life had she gone through moments like this alone, without someone to talk to? Too many to count. She had always handled things. She handled being a child and knowing the other students could hear the teacher. She had handled boarding school. She had handled her husband's rejection.

How would it feel to share her feelings with this man? She drew in a deep breath, because today wasn't the day. He was standing in front of her, but she couldn't let herself open up. She had to deal with it, figure it out, before she could share with someone else.

She couldn't get through this, trying to make sense of it, and worrying about how he would handle it.

"What are you doing here?"

"I couldn't let you do this alone."

"How did you know?"

"I overheard your conversation."

"Eavesdropping?" It was easier to smile than she would have imagined.

"Yeah, I guess. I meant to ignore it, to let it go. But I couldn't. I thought about it all day, about how you wanted to do everything alone, including this. But I couldn't let you."

"The boys?"

"With Janie."

Willow pushed the down button on the elevator. "Did you tell her where I am?"

"No, I didn't even tell her why I needed to come to Tulsa. I snooped and found the address in your office. Sorry about that."

He held out a handkerchief. She took it and brushed at her eyes, wiping away tears that hadn't fallen. She even smiled, because she could picture him in her office, peeking through papers.

"Sorry for which, for eavesdropping, snooping or following me?" She looked up at him.

He took the handkerchief and gently wiped under her eyes before handing it back to her. She held it, staring at the mascara stains, and wishing her heart wasn't melting. The duct tape she'd used to put it back together was coming apart at the seams, and she wanted to give a little of herself to a man who carried handkerchiefs and took the time to snoop through her papers.

"Should I apologize for trying to be a friend?"

She shook her head, but she couldn't answer, not without crying. She didn't want to cry. A few tears had leaked out, but she could hold it together. She didn't want to be the woman he pitied.

He touched her back and guided her through the open doors of the elevator. Once inside they stood at the back, shoulders touching. She had needed a friend, God had sent one, and the one He had sent was willing to wait, to not push for answers

"Do you want to talk?" Clint looked straight ahead, that straw hat pulled down over his eyes.

Her hand slid into his. "I can't talk about it right now. But I'm glad you're here."

She wasn't alone. Clint's hand squeezed lightly, and she didn't pull away. His hand holding hers convinced her that maybe, just maybe, he was someone she could let into her life.

The elevators touched the ground floor, and the doors slid open. They walked out together, no longer touching, and fingers no longer interlocked. Reality, a nice guy who knew she needed a friend.

"Would you like lunch before we drive home?" Clint asked as he walked by her side, into bright sunshine.

"I'm not hungry."

He nodded and led her across the parking lot to her truck. As they stood at the door she realized he had asked her another question, more words she hadn't heard.

"I'm sorry, what?" She couldn't make eye contact, so she stared down at her purse and the handkerchief.

"Are you going to be able to drive?"

She nodded and looked up. "Of course. I'm fine."

Always fine. But Clint didn't look like he believed her. As much as she wanted to tell him what the doctor had said, she couldn't, not yet. She wanted to hold on to hope for as long as possible.

She stood on tiptoe and kissed his cheek. "Thank you for being here."

"I haven't done much."

"You were here, and you didn't have to be." She filed that thought and knew she had to return to it later.

"I'll follow you." He pulled his keys out of his pocket and stood, waiting, like he wanted her to say more.

She shook her head. "You go on. I have to pick up a few things here."

As he started to turn, she caught hold of his arm. "Clint, thank you."

He smiled and walked away. She hoped he believed her. She had needed him. Now she needed to be alone for a while.

Clint walked out of the barn the next morning, hearing laughter and Willow's husky, alto voice. She had both boys on the swing that hung from an old oak in Janie's front yard. It was the kind of swing kids used to love, just a board strung on thick rope and tied to a sturdy branch. It was the kind of swing that made a kid think he was flying.

It was wide enough for both boys. They were leaning back, legs out, as they soared into the air. Willow caught them as they came down and gave them another push.

"Swing your legs out." She laughed as she coached them. "Make it go higher."

Had she ever been a child like that, carefree, swinging into the air, pretending she was flying? He hadn't been that kid. Most of the time he'd spent worrying about his parents, or his sister.

Now he worried about the boys. And Jenna. Because when she called, just before leaving Missouri, she had sounded scared, but she hadn't admitted to fear. Willow and his sister were a lot alike.

He crossed the lawn, Willow's dog nipping at his boots, asking for attention. He took a minute to toss the stick the dog had picked up and then he moved on. The boys called out to him, waving as they made another trip heavenward. Willow stepped back, smiling, but not at him.

She wasn't ready to talk about yesterday. He knew better than to push. Better to talk about the trip they were taking next week.

"When do we leave for Kansas City?" He leaned against the tree, out of the way of the swing.

"Next Thursday. I want to be there early enough for the bulls to settle in and settle down."

"The boys?" He didn't want to ask that of her, didn't want to ask in front of them. "I can drive my own truck."

"Nonsense, we can all ride together." She nodded toward the big old diesel that she drove to larger events. How many women would drive a truck like that? "I have a DVD player in my truck. We can bring movies."

"That sounds good. We can take turns driving." He knew better than to tell her he would drive.

Her gaze remained on him as he spoke, and she didn't turn away until she thought the conversation was over. She nodded, and even smiled a little, because she had to know that he was being careful not to step on her toes.

For her sake he wanted to believe everything was okay, as she insisted. He didn't believe it, though, not with shadows lingering in her eyes and her smile melting away when she thought no one was watching.

She smiled at the boys as they came back to ground. The twins jumped off the swing and walked unsteadily as they adjusted to being on land again. She didn't hear them talking to her. Clint touched her arm, and signed, repeating their question about the pony in the field.

He wondered why she had a pony, but didn't ask, because her eyes narrowed, and she bit down on her bottom lip as her gaze studied the two little boys. They had turned and were waiting for an answer.

She should have kids, he thought. She should have

five or six, and someone in her life taking care of her. He smiled at that, because he knew she didn't want to be taken care of, not in a coddling sort of way.

She was strong enough to hook a stock trailer to a truck and drive cross-country with a load of bulls. She was strong enough to start over after a marriage that had obviously hurt her.

What had happened yesterday at the doctor?

If he asked, she'd shut him out, so he didn't ask. And she was answering the boys, telling them they could ride the pony.

"Where did you get a pony?" He followed the woman and two boys to the barn.

"I bought him at an auction, half-starved and pitiful."

"And you needed a pony?"

She headed for the tack room, next to her office. Music played, and a horse in one of the stalls whinnied a greeting to them. This was the kind of barn a cowboy dreamed about, the kind he dreamed of.

Willow, unaware of his mental wanderings, opened the door to the tack room and flipped on the light. Inside were several saddles, halters and bridles hung on the walls, and saddle blankets were lined up along a board that had been nailed along one side of the room.

She turned back to face him. He realized she hadn't heard the pony question.

"You needed a pony?"

"I couldn't let him be sold to the…" She smiled at the boys and didn't finish her explanation for why she bought the pony. But he knew what companies bought sick old ponies at auctions, and he would have done the same thing she had.

It was one more thing he knew about her. She rescued sad animals. And cowboys who had no place to go. He glanced down at his nephews. And she rescued little boys who had to say goodbye to their mother.

"Who rescues you, Willow?" The words were out before he could stop them. And she had heard.

She turned, her head tilted to the side. She had just pulled a tiny saddle out of the tack room and she set it on a rail, a miniature bridle hooked over the saddle horn.

"What does *that* mean?"

He shrugged and resisted the urge to be a coward and run. Instead he picked denial. "Nothing."

"It meant something."

"Okay, it meant something. I guess I don't want to talk about it any more than you want to talk about your doctor's appointment yesterday."

She smiled, a little sad and a little proud.

"I rescue myself, Clint."

The answer he had expected from her. "Fair enough."

"Come on, guys. Let's go ride Tiny Boy. And then we can brush him and give him grain."

Because riding was about learning responsibility. He smiled as he followed her to the end of the barn and through the double doors that led to the field. She carried the saddle and ignored him, sending an obvious message that he didn't fail to understand. He knew the most important thing about her.

She rescued herself.

## Chapter Seven

The Kansas City event was one that Willow loved. It was huge. It was close to home. And people knew her. She had friends here. As she walked through the wide halls toward the arena and the area where the bulls were penned and waiting, she managed to push aside the fear that had reared its ugly head when her doctor left a message the previous day that she needed to call him.

She hadn't called. She'd do that when she got home. This weekend she would take care of business. She would watch her bulls perform, and she'd visit with friends. What she wouldn't do was let her peace be stolen away.

Next week she'd deal with reality.

Tonight's reality was a pen holding her bulls, bulls she'd raised and trained herself. She had earned the right to supply these animals to some of the biggest bull-riding and rodeo events in the country.

She wouldn't feel bad about her life and her accomplishments. She wouldn't lose faith.

Arms crossed over the top rail of the pen, she watched the bulls, thinking about the animals, her life here, and the life she'd left behind. It felt good to be happy, to be content. It felt good to be in control. No matter what.

"Feels good, doesn't it." Clint was at her side. "You've done a great job with these bulls."

"It does feel good. It's something I've done for myself. I'm not doing it for my dad, or for Brad. It hasn't been given to me." She turned, smiling because she had given more of an answer than she'd planned to give. He was good at disarming her. "No one can take it away from me."

"No one can."

No one could take it away from her. But she could lose it all if her hearing loss continued to escalate. Eventually she would have to tell the people in her life. She would have to admit that she couldn't always hear the announcer calling the names of the bulls, or the riders. She couldn't hear when her name was called because her bull had won certain challenges.

She would have to admit to herself that she needed help. And then she would admit it to Janie, and to Clint.

"I'm going to talk to Bailey. Have you seen Janie?" She unhooked her arm from the fence and turned, facing him.

"She's with the boys. Cody Jacobs brought a horse with him, and they're taking turns riding."

"Okay, then I'll catch up with you in a little while."

He nodded and she walked away. Bailey was easy to find. She was at the edge of the arena, watching her husband give the twins a ride on his big buckskin gelding. His daughter, Meg, stood at his side. Willow approached her friend, remembering how they met and how hard it was for Bailey and Cody to let go of the past and find a future together.

And Willow had helped to bring them together. She had helped in their happy-ever-after, even though she hadn't believed in one for herself.

"Willow, you look gorgeous." Bailey moved toward her, hands coming out to take Willow's.

And Bailey glowed. Willow's gaze lingered on the other woman's belly. The rumors were true. "Oh, Bailey, you should have told me."

"I wanted to wait until I saw you. I wanted to tell you in person." Bailey's smile was soft. "Willow, I…"

"Please don't, Bailey. This is your moment. I'm your friend, and I want this for you."

Willow hugged her, holding her tight. When they stepped away from one another, Willow smiled, wanting to prove her words. It wouldn't hurt.

"When are you due?"

"Six months."

"I guess it's too soon to know if it's a boy or girl."

Bailey laughed, "Yes, way too soon."

"How is Meg taking this? Is she excited?"

"She's excited, and then she starts thinking about sharing her parents, and sharing her puppy. As quickly as she thinks of those things, she starts thinking of plans for what she's going to teach the baby."

"Do you have names picked?"

Bailey laughed at that, a real laugh, the kind that made people turn to look at them. "Meg likes the name Dolly, after your bull. She thinks we should name her brother, if the baby's a boy, *Dolly*. Thank you for that."

Willow laughed with her friend, and when the laughter ended, Bailey reached for her hand. "How did your doctor's appointment go? I wish you would have said something sooner. I would have gone with you."

"I know you would have. But really, I'm used to it." Used to being alone. She shook the thought from her mind.

A movement caught Willow's attention. She glanced up, making eye contact with Clint, standing near the gate. He smiled, and she felt it, almost as if he had reached out and touched her.

His fingers moved, asking if she was okay. And she was, of course she was. Why would he ask that? She ignored the question and he walked toward them, his walk a casual, cowboy swagger.

"Is there something going on that I should know about?" Bailey smiled, her eyes shifting from Clint to Willow.

"You know there isn't. He's helping me, and we're helping him with the boys."

"He got hurt a couple of weeks ago, didn't he?" Bailey smiled at Clint, who was nearly to them.

"Yes, he dislocated his shoulder."

Clint stopped in front of them. He smiled at Bailey and held out his hand. "Clint Cameron."

"Bailey Jacobs. Nice to meet you, Clint."

"Willow, that young bull is a little droopy, and he isn't drinking water."

"He likes bottled water. I think the chlorine in city water makes him sick. I should have told you." She stepped away, giving Bailey an apologetic smile. "I need to check on him. But we'll have dinner tomorrow night?"

"Of course."

"Okay, then, I'd better go." Willow walked away, knowing that Clint was on her heels. She felt him there, his arm brushing hers as he caught up.

"You okay?"

"Of course I'm okay. Why did you think I wasn't okay? And that bull had better be sick." Not that she wanted the bull to be sick. "I mean, I hope you didn't make that up."

He laughed and shook his head. "The bull is sick, and your face was pale. You looked like you were trying to be happy."

"I *was* trying to be happy. Is there something wrong with trying to be happy for a friend?"

"Nothing at all. I just thought you looked upset."

Willow sighed and turned to face him. It was crowded, and he moved her to the side. "Do you think she thought I was upset? I would never want her to think that I wasn't happy for her."

"She didn't notice."

Willow bit down on her bottom lip. "Bailey and Cody deserve to be happy."

Willow's phone rang a few times as she approached the bull pen. It vibrated in her pocket, and she pulled it out and flipped it open. Her attention was on the sick bull, and the caller's voice faded in and out.

"I'm sorry, I didn't catch that." She held the phone tight and blocked the sounds of the arena, where people milled, checking on bulls and talking about the event.

The caller repeated the question, but she only caught that he wanted information. Clint moved in front of her, signing that he could take the call.

Because she couldn't. And she knew it. She shouldn't be angry with him, it wasn't his fault. She didn't want him to think she needed him or anyone else to take over because she couldn't handle it. She didn't want to give up. Would he understand that she had to keep trying, and hoping it would work?

With Clint watching, she gave the caller her e-mail address and explained that her connection was bad and there was too much noise in the arena.

She hung up and slipped the phone back into her pocket.

"I could have taken that call for you." Clint rested one foot on the bottom rail of the pen that held her bulls.

"Yes, you could have, but I didn't want you to. I handled it."

"Yes, you handled it."

She looked at the young bull, only his second time at an event this size. He didn't look good. She didn't like to think that he could really be sick.

"We should call the vet."

"Do you want to do that?" Clint continued to stare at the bull. His hands moved deftly, and she nodded in answer.

Sign language was just easier sometimes. Signs didn't have to compete with the commotion of the arena. Signs weren't overheard. And he knew that. He couldn't know that there were times she couldn't hear him.

Or maybe he did.

"Willow, what's up?"

She closed her eyes and leaned her forehead against the top rail of the pen. "I'm sorry. There's so much going on, and you're here, and you don't deserve to catch the brunt of it all."

"I can handle it."

She didn't know if *she* could handle it. "Thanks. I would appreciate it if you would call the vet. I need to see what Janie is up to. And I'll take the boys with me. If you want?"

"That would be great."

Yes, it would. For the next few hours, until the event started, she could be distracted by Janie and the boys. She could keep her mind off babies, sick bulls and the competition.

Later tonight she would be alone, and then, in the privacy of her room, she could fall apart.

\* \* \*

After Willow walked away, Clint went to the locker room to call the vet, and to get ready. He had wanted a last-minute prayer, a quick check of his equipment, and what he'd gotten instead was a conversation with Cody Jacobs.

Clint left the locker room and walked through the narrow hall leading to the arena, his bull rope dragging behind him with the bell clanking against the concrete floor. He needed his mind on the ride against a bull that should be a sure thing, and not on the magazine article that Cody had shown him, an article about a deaf woman raising bulls, and the abuse of the animals.

Cody had, for some reason, seen Clint as the person who needed to know, the person to handle the problem. Like Willow was his to handle, or protect. Clint had wanted to explain to Cody about his dad, his sister in Iraq and the twins. He had almost asked Cody Jacobs if he understood what it meant to have a full plate.

Instead he had agreed that someone needed to break the news to Willow. And he was the guy. The guy who was going to have to hurt her, and he knew she was already hurting. He didn't look forward to telling her.

At least she had the good news that her bull wasn't sick, just cranky and in a bad mood. He sort of understood how that bull felt. He was a little cranky himself.

When his bull was in the chute and ready, someone called out to him. It was Jason Bradshaw. The two had never run in the same circles. But Bradshaw was a good guy and a good neighbor.

"I'll pull your rope, Clint." Jason stood on the outside of the chute, ready to help.

They were in the same circle now. Bull riding had a way of breaking down social barriers. On the back of a bull, it wasn't about where you grew up or what your savings account looked like. The bull didn't care.

The crowd cheering from the stands didn't care.

"Thanks, Bradshaw." Clint fastened his Kevlar vest and pulled his hat down tight. He climbed over the gate and settled on the broad back of the bull.

"Mammas Don't Let Your Babies Grow Up to Be Cowboys" was the song blasting from the speakers, and over the snort of the bull and the steady stream of conversation around him, he could hear the crowds singing the chorus of the song. He could hear the heavy breathing of the bull and the clang of metal as the animal pushed into the gate.

A glance to the side, and he saw Willow talking to Bailey but watching him. Funny how life had thrown them together, the princess and the pauper. He smiled as he slid his hand into the bull rope, because he knew they weren't a fairy tale, just two people who would have something in common for a short time.

Bull riding smudged lines and brought people together. But that didn't mean they were in each other's lives.

He found his seat on the back of the bull, distracted, and he knew better. The bull was steady, calm, he'd done this before. Clint bowed his head and said a quick prayer, wound the bull rope around his gloved riding hand and nodded for the gate to open.

A bull that was a sure thing, an easy ninety-point ride. Clint made all the right moves, doing his best to make a good ride even better. He used his free arm to keep in the center. He kept his gaze focused forward, on the bull's head, and he kept his toes pointing out. As the buzzer sounded the end of eight seconds, he jumped, but miscalculated and hit the gate, his head connecting first, and then his shoulder. Or maybe it was simultaneous.

Fire shot through his shoulder, and he slumped to the ground, not even caring that the bull raced past him. Jim Dandy wasn't a mean bull, had never been mean.

A bullfighter held a hand out, and Clint took it.

"Thanks." Clint rubbed the back of his head.

"You okay?" One of the sports medicine team had joined them.

Clint nodded, and it hurt. All over.

"I think he hit his head on the gate and scattered his chickens." The bull-fighter pounded Clint on the back, chuckled and walked away.

Clint cringed because it had done more than scatter his chickens. He could almost imagine the questions people would ask, about why a cowboy kept trying to ride the bull. He didn't have an answer, but he knew that it was about competing with something wild. Man against beast, a battle as old as time.

Some men chased tornadoes, others jumped from

planes. He rode bulls, sometimes for eight seconds, and sometimes not.

He stood and tipped his hat to the cheering crowd as the medics followed him out of the arena and through the building to their temporary examining room—heavy curtains hung on bars to give the riders a little privacy.

"Have a seat, Clint." The physician, a man in his sixties, pointed to a table covered with sheets of white paper.

"Do I have to? I'm sure it's fine." Sore, but fine. He had to be fine.

"How about if you let me be the doctor, and you be the bull rider. We'll both be better off for it." Doc Clemens smiled as he lifted Clint's arm at an angle that didn't feel too good. "Hmm."

"What's 'hmmm' mean?"

"It means that I don't think you should ride, but I also don't think you're going to listen to me. It means that I can't be sure until further examination, but I think you're finally going to need surgery."

"Hmmm." Clint smiled and then grimaced when one of the medics placed a bag of ice on his shoulder. "That's cold."

"I think you should call it a weekend."

"I can't. If I can win…"

"Yes, *if* you can win. There's always that elusive *if*." The older doctor was a little less than pleasant when it came to bedside manner. "If you want, we can try tying it down. Sometimes it works."

His elbow tied to his waist to keep him from moving his arm straight up. He'd be able to move it just enough to keep it in the air, away from the bull and the automatic disqualification if he touched the animal. He shook his head, not sure if he liked the idea.

A commotion outside and men clearing a path interrupted the conversation. Willow kept her gaze on him as she walked through the room.

"Don't be stupid, Clint." She smiled at the doctor, who went a little red in the face. "If you can't ride, you can't ride."

"I can ride. It's my free arm."

"Which you need for balance."

He shot a look over her shoulder in time to see a few of the guys laugh and shake their heads. This he didn't need. And if she'd been thinking, she would know she didn't need it, either. She had just added to the rumor that had been started by the magazine article. Not that she had any way of knowing about the magazine.

But after the interview she'd made it pretty clear she didn't want her name linked with his.

"Willow, I'm going to make the right decision for me."

And for his family. The weekend had a big purse at stake, and that money would go a long way in building his dream. It was money that would put up fences and buy cattle.

"What about the boys?" She looked around a little nervously, as if she had just realized where she was and who all was watching. Calm, cool and detached crumbled across her face, and she bit down on her bottom lip, suddenly vulnerable.

He wanted to pull her close and tell her it would all work out. But he couldn't make those promises to her.

"Everything I do is for my family." He spoke a little softer and started to reach for her hand. Instead he winked as if he didn't feel a need to convince her he was okay. "Don't worry, I've been hurt a lot worse than this."

"Okay, well then, I guess I'm going back out there. Janie has the boys already tucked in, so you can crash and not worry about them."

She nodded and walked away, not giving him time to respond, to argue, or to even ask her how her bulls had done. And since Doc Clemens was about to stick a huge needle in his shoulder, it didn't seem to matter.

## Chapter Eight

Willow left Clint and walked down the hall, back to the crowds gathered behind the chutes. Several stock contractors smiled, a few riders nodded in her direction. They all seemed to be whispering. And she seemed to be the center of attention.

The center of attention was exactly where she didn't want to be. She avoided that place, the place where people stared and whispered.

It could be about anything. It could be that they were already discussing the fact that she stomped into the examining room and confronted Clint as if she had a right.

She tried to tell herself that she was used to people staring and talking about her in quiet whispers. Not here, though, in this sport where she'd been accepted. One of the contractors left his group of friends and headed in her direction.

"How ya doin', Willow?" Dan slapped a rolled-up magazine against his thigh and sighed.

"I thought I was fine, Dan. But from the look on your face, maybe I'm not?"

"Willow, I'm not going to beat around the bush. There's a pretty nasty article in this magazine. I have a feeling you haven't seen it."

She shook her head. No, she hadn't seen it. He handed it to her, and she unrolled it. Willow glanced at the cover, and then she understood the whispers, the curious glances. She flipped to the page of the article.

"I'm sorry, Willow."

She nodded as she skimmed the article, a story about a woman with a disability, and bulls being mistreated. She glanced at the bull in the chute and the cowboy sliding onto his back. The judge was there, making sure it didn't take too long for the cowboy to get settled and out the gate. That rule was meant to protect the animals and keep them safe from stress or injury.

And her own bulls, drinking bottled water and eating the best hay and grain available. She skimmed the article, stopping when she saw Clint's name. She groaned and shook her head.

"Great."

"It isn't the end of the world." Dan chuckled. "Shoot, Willow, there are plenty of couples around here that met at a bull ride. And Clint's a good guy."

"But it isn't true."

"Of course it isn't. But you're okay. You have good bulls, and nothing to be ashamed of. This isn't the first article written about bull riding, won't be the last.

This guy took his story to a personal level that wasn't really necessary."

She thanked Dan, smiling and shaking her head when he tried to give words of encouragement. As she walked away his words were indiscernible, but she caught something about it not being a big deal.

For her, it was a big deal. This was about her reputation. It was about people respecting her as a professional, not thinking of her as someone weak, someone who needed sympathy or help.

Ignoring Bailey, who waved from the sidelines, wanting to talk, Willow walked back to the area where temporary pens had been set up for the bulls. Her bulls were there, fed, cared for and healthy.

She ripped the pages out of the magazine and dropped them in a nearby trash barrel. The article was trash. And it felt good to watch the pages flutter down, finding a resting place with soda cans, wrappers from burgers, and popcorn.

"What are you doing?" Clint stood next to her, glancing into the trash barrel. She hadn't heard him walk up.

She shrugged and ripped more pages, feeling better already. "I'm not a victim. I'm not disabled. I'm a woman of faith. I'm strong. I take care of my animals."

"Okay."

She glanced up at him, smiling when he smiled, because she knew that she wasn't making sense. "Did you know about the magazine?"

"I did, and I was going to tell you."

"Were you working up the courage?"

He pointed to the bag of ice under his shirt. It had been taped to his shoulder with duct tape. "No, I was getting a shot in the arm."

"Do I really act like this person he portrayed me to be?" She hoped not.

She didn't want to discuss the money that had been the consolation prize at the end of a marriage. Or the husband who had used her father's name to build his own career in Washington.

Worse, what he'd said about her relationship with Clint. She had traded a privileged life in Washington for a cowboy with a fading dream of being a pro bull rider.

The article hadn't been kind to him, either.

Clint smiled, reassuring, calm. "You're not the person in that article. The divorce is behind you. It's a part of your past."

Heat crawled up her cheeks. "I was dumped for someone I thought was my best friend."

"I know." He shrugged his right shoulder. "And I have fading dreams of making it big."

"Your dreams aren't fading."

"No, they're not fading, just changing. I'm getting too old for this sport. But I'm going to rebuild that farm that's seen better days. And I could think of worse things than having my name connected to yours. Even if it is just a rumor."

She looked down, glancing at the few pages of the

magazine still intact, including a recipe for some mid-western-style casserole.

"Oh, wow, I want this recipe." She folded it up and put it in the pocket of her jeans.

"Changing the subject?"

"Maybe. I don't want to talk about this. I don't want to talk about what this says about us, or about my bulls or how I lucked into success."

Clint leaned close. He didn't touch her, and she wanted to be touched. "You didn't luck into it. You did this on your own. You're incredible."

She nodded, and then she backed away, because they were in a public place and they didn't need to feed the gossip that had already started.

"Thank you. I'm sorry for what the article says about you. It isn't true."

"I know."

She took a few more steps back. "I have to go."

Because there had to be lines, somewhere between them, lines they didn't cross. Because if they crossed the lines, and he became someone she counted on, how could she go back to not having him in her life?

She would handle it, because that's what she did. She had learned to handle things as a kid, moving from place to place, trying to make new friends, and losing good ones along the way. She handled life, and being alone. She handled men walking away.

She smiled, and he smiled back. "See you in the morning."

He reached for her hand. "Let's grab a cup of coffee and unwind. I won this round, and I'd like to celebrate."

A cup of coffee. Friendship. A man who understood that she was strong and she could survive. But he was also a rescuer. So was the coffee a lifeline, or friendship?

"Not tonight."

Tonight was a good night not to be rescued. Tonight she needed to keep her distance because there was a soft, vulnerable spot in her heart, and an ache to be held. She said goodbye and walked away. But behind her Clint was still standing by her bulls, and her heart was remembering how it felt to have lines crossed with a kiss.

Sunday morning, Willow walked down the steps to the small area of the stadium where church was being held. It was quiet—no bulls bellowed from the chutes and cowboys didn't line the platform, waiting to ride. Maybe a hundred people had gathered to worship. There were bull riders, stock contractors, family, and even a few spectators.

One of the guys played the guitar, signaling a start to the service. Willow sat at the back, not wanting to be a part of conversation or greetings. Today she wanted to be alone, to think about the future and why she was suddenly dreaming about a cowboy.

Janie had taken the boys to a local church, and then they were going to the zoo. They would make a real day of it, and the twins needed that. Clint had planned to sleep in, because pain meds did that to him, he'd explained.

Willow didn't feel abandoned. She needed time with God, to worship and to feel His presence. She had work to do on her heart that morning, and it had to do with anger toward the reporter. She'd lain in bed last night reliving the interview and what she should have said. And then moving on to what she'd say if she ever saw that guy again.

Real anger, real emotion, the kind that if it wasn't controlled could get a person in real trouble. She smiled at the thought but then reminded herself again how wrong it would be to say the things she wanted to say.

The song service started. Willow stood, closing her eyes to listen because the guitar was soft and the voices were strong. She sang along, enjoying that moment when the world slipped away and she was alone with God. And since God was the only one close enough to hear, she didn't mind singing out loud.

Alone with God, and then a soft breeze and mountain pine cologne. A shoulder touched hers. She opened her eyes, and Clint smiled down at her. She closed her eyes again, not wanting to be distracted, and knowing how easily it could happen.

The music ended, and they sat down together. The speaker for the day was one of the bull riders. He opened his Bible and announced a passage of scripture. Willow flipped through her Bible, looking, but missing the chapters. She had sat too far back to read lips, and too far to catch everything he said.

And it was her own fault, for being stubborn, for wanting to be alone. Two months ago it wouldn't have been an issue. Now, now everything was different.

Clint reached for her Bible and pointed to the correct passage. *And the peace of God, which passeth all understanding, shall keep your hearts and minds through Christ Jesus.*

She read the verses above and the ones that came after, and then she lingered again on *peace. Not* as the world gives it, but peace that is real. Not found in things, not found in circumstances, or in perfect moments, but peace found in God.

The speaker's hushed tones didn't quite reach, but Willow didn't care, God had already spoken to her heart in those verses.

Clint touched her arm as she strained to hear, and then his hands moved, signing the sermon, deftly, quietly, just for her. And he didn't know what the doctor had told her, or the uncertainty of the future. She blinked against the sting of tears, and her eyes blurred as she watched his hands.

Hands that rode bulls, hugged little boys, fixed fences, and now, spoke the words of God for her.

When the sermon ended, Willow signed THANK YOU, just for him, between the two of them. And then she reached for his hand and pulled it to her lips. A brief kiss, something to let him know how his kindness touched her.

"I have to go now." She slid past him, not wanting to wait, to explain, or to have him tell her he understood. He wouldn't be able to understand what she couldn't begin to fathom about herself, her life or her feelings.

He reached for her hand as she started up the steps, and she stopped.

"Willow, we both have to eat lunch."

Simple, nonintrusive lunch.

She had a list of reasons why she had to walk away, and for a moment they seemed meaningless. To be honest, she couldn't remember a single one of those reasons.

"Okay, lunch is good."

He stood up, grinning, and then he winked. "Say it like you mean it."

"I mean it." And suddenly she did, because his hand reached for hers, warm, calloused and strong, and he was a friend.

"I'm buying."

"I can buy my own lunch."

"I know you can, but I'm not going to let you."

And that made it feel too much like a date, too much like a line crossed. But a strong person could let a man buy her lunch and not be frightened by tomorrow, or next week, or even next year.

It's just lunch, Willow. He had pulled his hand free and signed the words, keeping it between them and not the people walking up behind them.

"I know."

"Tell me one really embarrassing thing about yourself. Something really private."

Willow pulled away, ready to think up an excuse, a reason she needed out of this lunch date, and then she saw his smile. He winked and pulled her close again.

"Kidding, Willow. Nothing embarrassing or private, not today."

"No, I like that idea. But today, you have to tell me something about yourself, too."

They were walking down a hallway lit by fluorescent lights, toward the exit at the back of the building, and somehow they had lost the others from the church service. Or maybe they'd gone a different way. Willow hadn't really been paying attention. Instead she felt a little lost in the lighthearted moment between herself and a cowboy in new jeans and a white button-down shirt, the sleeves rolled up to expose blond hair on suntanned arms.

He was the kind of cowboy a girl could lose her heart to. The kind dreams were made of.

He pushed the doors open and motioned for her to go through. They walked across the parking lot, not talking. It reminded her of the day at the doctor's office when he hadn't pushed for her secrets.

"You go first." She smiled, not looking at him, but wondering what was in his mind, and what face he was making.

"First?" He was pulling the keys to the truck out of his pocket.

"Secret sharing, remember?"

"Okay, I'll go first."

Curious, she looked up, and he smiled, his eyes crinkling at the corners. He had pushed his hands into his pockets, and he pulled them out, signing as he spoke.

"I sucked my thumb until I was four."

And she could picture that, because she knew that he must have looked like David. An insecure little boy with silver-blond hair and gray eyes. And now, insecure? She didn't think so.

"That isn't embarrassing." She opened the passenger-side door, even though he was there. "That's cute."

"Cute, huh?" He laughed. "So you think I'm cute?"

"Four-year-old Clint, with blond hair and torn jeans, his thumb in his mouth, was cute. You're…"

His brows arched, waiting.

"You're too full of yourself."

"You still think I'm cute."

"For a dirty ole bull rider, who limps a lot and creaks when he stands up, I guess you're okay."

"So, now it's your turn." He was leaning in, one hand on the door to keep it from blowing shut. Up close she could see the crinkles at the corners of his eyes and a tiny cut on his forehead from the fall last night.

"I don't think so. You gave me thumb sucking, which isn't private or embarrassing."

His smile faded and he looked at her, a long look that made her doubt whether she should push him for personal information.

"Never mind."

No, I'll give you something. He signed, slower now, more thoughtful. She stopped his hands, holding them in hers.

"I can hear you."

"Okay. I've never really been in love. A couple of times I thought I might be, but it never worked out." He shrugged.

And Willow had been right; she was sorry that she'd pushed him to reveal his stories. It was too much information, and in his eyes she could still see that boy who had been hurt too many times.

Sharing secrets was dangerous. It had opened a door that shouldn't have been opened.

"Too much information?" He smiled and when he climbed in behind the wheel, he shot her a look. "Your turn."

"I'm not sure if I made that deal." She clicked her seatbelt and reached to turn the radio down.

"I think we did." He started the truck and shifted into reverse. "Come on, if I can share that I'm a dropout in the school of love, surely you can give me something."

"You want me to share something miserable about my life, so you can feel better about yours?" She couldn't help but smile.

"Something like that."

"Okay, I won't go into detail, but I, too, am a—what did you call it?"

"Dropout in the school of love."

"Catchy, in a tongue-tying sort of way. Okay, I'm

the girl most likely to be standing alone at any social function because people think I can't communicate. And I'm the most likely to be dumped." She could have told him the many different ways she'd been dumped or stood up. But that was a little too much reality for a beautiful summer day.

He winked. "At least we have each other."

"Of course. Now, if you think we've sufficiently humiliated ourselves, I would really like pizza."

His eyebrows arched. "Pizza it is."

Step one in developing a new life— Try new things.

She smiled at Clint and he smiled back. And it felt a lot like trying something new.

Clint's phone rang just as he was paying the waitress for their lunch. He answered and listened as Janie explained that David had fallen asleep on the way back to the hotel from church, and he was crying for his mom. They hadn't made it to the zoo.

When they walked through the door of Willow's suite at the hotel, Clint saw David sitting in a corner of the couch, tears still streaming down his face. Willow made a noise, and he turned. Her eyes shimmered with tears and she gave him a watery smile.

"I'll take Timmy downstairs for ice cream," she offered.

"No, don't. I'm not sure what to say to him, Willow. I don't know how to get him through this."

"Pray with him, Clint. That's the only answer. He's a little boy, but a child's faith is stronger than you think." She smiled past him, at the child on the couch, hugging knees to his chest. "And hug him."

He nodded, but it took him back more than twenty years, to his own mother sitting on his bed praying for him to make wise decisions. He had forgotten. How had he forgotten something so important?

He also remembered how it had felt when she didn't come home that first night after the accident. His world had shattered, and he'd had to pick up his own pieces, and Jenna's, too, because their father hadn't been able.

He did have an idea of how Timmy and David felt. They were younger than he had been, but he had experienced those empty nights of waiting for someone to come home. Jenna would come back.

Willow touched his back and when he turned, she smiled. "Do you want me to stay?"

He did. But he shook his head. "No, I should handle this one. I'll take both boys to my room. And then they should probably take a nap before tonight."

"Are you riding tonight?"

He shook his head. "No, I'm not going to take that chance."

"I'm sorry."

He shrugged, and he was sorry, too. It was his dream slipping away. He had a feeling she understood.

"I'll catch up with you later." He gathered the boys and headed for the doors. "I'll help you with the bulls tonight, since I won't have anything else to do."

The boys leaned against him, a little weepy and a little tired. Just boys in need of one-on-one time. He held them close and walked them to the door. Willow stood to the side, and he remembered what she'd told him about herself, that a lot of her life she had stood by herself in a hearing world, feeling different.

## Chapter Nine

Tuesday morning, Willow fed her animals early and headed for the house to talk to Janie. On the drive home from Kansas City she had prayed about talking to her aunt. She wanted Janie to keep her dream of moving to Florida. First Willow had to convince Janie that she'd be able to run the ranch without her aunt to help.

When she walked into the kitchen, Janie turned from taking the newly baked biscuits from the baking sheet. She didn't smile. Not good.

"What's up?" Willow leaned against the counter, watching her aunt.

"I have a message from your doctor for you. He wants you to call." Janie frowned again. "You went to the doctor?"

"I did, and he did tests."

"And?"

"And, I don't know. I haven't talked to him yet."

Willow poured herself a cup of coffee that smelled old, but she didn't really want to drink it. She wanted something to distract herself. "Janie, I don't want to talk about it. I'll call him, and I'll find out what the test results were."

Big sigh from Janie. "Okay, but you have to let me know what he says."

"I will." Willow smiled, and then she wrapped her aunt in a loose hug. "Janie, I know you want to move to Florida, and I want you to sell me the ranch. Or at least let me lease it."

Janie pulled loose from the hug. "Don't butter me up with hugs, Willow. I'm worried, and you want to sidetrack me with this conversation."

"I'm not buttering you up. I put it off, and now seems like a good time to talk. You want to move. And I don't want you to stay here, believing you have to take care of me."

Janie shook her head. "You know that I don't think that."

Willow sipped the burnt coffee and then poured it down the sink. It was past disgusting. "You would stay for that reason. I can hire Clint. And I have Brian."

"I know you do. But you're my girl, and I don't want to leave you alone."

"If you don't go, you'll regret it, and I'll feel guilty."

Janie nodded. "I'll think about it. The girls are flying down to Florida in two weeks. I might just go with them. If you think you'll be okay."

"I'll be okay. And now, I need to go talk to Clint. I

need to make sure he's willing to help. If not, I'll put the word out that I'm looking for a foreman."

"Clint would be a great choice. The two of you…"

Willow raised a hand. "Don't go there, Janie. Clint is a friend, and that's all. I'm not looking for anything more than friendship. I've learned my lesson."

"We all have lessons to learn. We never stop learning, and we should never stop growing. But we should also keep the doors open so that God can do what He wants to do in our lives."

"I'll remember that." Willow grabbed a biscuit off the baking sheet and blew a kiss to her aunt. "I'll be back."

As Willow walked toward the foreman's house, she tossed the last bite of biscuit to Bell, who trotted along behind her, stubby tail wagging. Willow could smell bacon frying.

As Willow walked up the stairs to the front porch of the house, she heard Clint singing along to the radio. The boys were laughing. She stopped, not wanting to interrupt.

She leaned against the side of the house, listening to something beautiful. The laughter of the children, the love in Clint's voice when he told Timmy to get ready for a great breakfast, and country music filtering out the screen door. She hugged herself, wishing for something she couldn't have and knowing that soon she might not be able to hear moments like this.

"Oh man, this isn't good," Clint shouted. The boys screamed. She couldn't make out all of their words.

Time to interrupt. Willow knocked on the door, and

he yelled for her to come in. She walked into the kitchen and into chaos. The skillet was on fire. Clint was slapping it with a wet towel. The boys were standing against the far wall, hands over their mouths.

"The lid, Clint." Willow walked across the room, searching the counter. No lid. She grabbed a baking sheet out of the dish drainer and slid it over the top of the pan, smothering the flames.

Clint dropped the singed towel in the sink, and then he rubbed his shoulder. "I'm not a cook."

"Obviously. But what have you done all these years, because you're definitely not starving?"

"Drive-thru, what else?" He smiled. "What has you down here so bright and early?"

"I guess I'm here to tell the boys that I can make decent scrambled eggs." She looked into the pan. "But the bacon is a lost cause."

"I can help." Clint grinned, and the boys groaned.

"I think that's a response you can't ignore. Timmy and David have vetoed your offer." She grabbed the carton of eggs and a bowl out of the dish drainer. "Do you have milk?"

Clint pulled a half-full jug out of the fridge. "Milk. What else?"

"Cheese?"

He found cheese and tossed the bag next to the milk. "What are you doing here so early, other than making breakfast for three starving guys?"

"Did I say I would make you breakfast? I think I just offered to make breakfast for the boys."

"You wouldn't let me starve."

"No, I wouldn't." She cracked eggs into the bowl. "I came down to talk to you about working for me. Permanently. Janie and I discussed her move to Florida. I don't want her to feel like she has to stay here and take care of me."

"You know that I want to work on my farm."

"I know. And I really can put out the word that I need to hire someone. It's just that you…"

She sighed, because it was a lot to tell him. He made her feel comfortable. And he knew sign language. The comfort part was easy to admit. But if she admitted the part about sign language it meant admitting something more about herself and her future.

"Willow, I do want to work for you. I only mean to say that I can work here, and I can work on my place. I can do both."

"I don't want to take you away from something that's important to you."

"You won't be taking me away." He took the lid off the milk and handed it to her. "We work well together. I don't think you're going to find anyone else quite like me."

She smiled up at him. "I can't imagine that I would."

Timmy and David gathered at her side, watching as she cracked eggs into the bowl. They were still wearing pajamas, and they hadn't brushed their hair. Their uncle had the same, hadn't-been-up-long look. She glanced sideways at the man next to her in sweats cut off at the knees, bare feet and a white T-shirt.

"Can we help?" Timmy looked into the bowl.

Distracted, she nodded, and then she had to admit she hadn't really heard his question. He gave her a look and repeated it.

"You can." Willow handed him the whisk. "Can you mix this up for me?"

The little boy stirred and stirred until the eggs were foamy and splattering on the counter.

"I think that's good." Clint took the whisk and handed it to David. "Your turn."

David stirred, more gently. He kept hold of his bottom lip with his teeth, concentrating. Willow leaned and kissed the top of his head. She prayed for their mom, that Jenna would come home soon.

And she prayed for herself, because she had to call the doctor and face her own future. They were all facing changes. She wrapped an arm around Timmy and he cuddled into her side.

She wouldn't have traded that morning with them for anything.

After breakfast Clint watched Willow heading for the barn, the twins walking with her. She had a surprise for them. He knew that it was a calf from a local dairy farm. She'd bought it for the boys to bottle-feed.

He cleaned the kitchen, washing the skillet the eggs had been cooked in and leaving the bacon pan to soak. As he walked down toward the barn, Bell joined him, carrying the ever-present stick in her mouth. He tossed it and kept walking.

Squeals of delight echoed in the early morning, and somewhere a rooster crowed, a little late. Clint walked around the side of the barn and saw the boys standing in front of the corral, both holding tight to the giant-sized bottle that they held through the fence for the calf.

The calf pushed again, like he would have done to his mom's udder, trying to get more milk. The boys laughed, real belly laughs. The calf pushed the bottle, and they dropped it on the ground. Timmy held out his hand, and the calf slid a long tongue over the boy's fingers.

Clint leaned against the corner of the barn and watched Willow. She was leaning against the fence, gazing at the boys. Her hair was pulled back in a ponytail, and her blue eyes shimmered. When she saw him, she smiled, a smile that didn't hold back, that didn't have shadows.

David had picked up the bottle, and the calf sucked again, just getting air. The boys groaned because they didn't want to stop feeding the calf. And the calf wasn't ready for them to stop.

"We'll give him grain, guys. He won't be hungry." Willow took the slobbery bottle and held it loosely in one hand. Clint laughed, because she owned bucking bulls, and she was holding that bottle like it was a bug.

"Want me to take that?" he offered.

She tossed it, and he had to catch it or get hit. His hand slid down the side, and the calf slobber slimed him. Okay, it wasn't pleasant. He looked up, and she was giving him a look, brows raised and a little quirk to her lips.

"What's the matter, is it disgusting?" she asked as she handed the feed bucket to the boys. Timmy held the handle and climbed the fence to dump it into the feeder.

David grabbed the water hose.

Clint shrugged. "Doesn't bother me at all. What did you name the calf?"

"Sir Loin," the boys shouted in unison.

"Nice." Clint shook his head. "I'm not going to ask."

"It was a tough choice." Willow grinned. "Sir Loin, or T Bone."

"Cute." He didn't mean the name of the cow, but she didn't have to know. "Do you mind if the boys stay here with you while I work on my place?"

She shook her head. "Not at all. We're going to drive down the road to look at the neighbor's new puppies."

"New puppies?" He had a bad feeling about this.

"Don't look so worried. They won't be weaned for a few weeks."

"I'm not worried." But he was. Not about the puppies, but about his sister, his nephews and Willow. "I'll see you later. I'll be at the farm if you need me."

He walked away from Willow and realized that was what bothered him. He was having a hard time walking away from her. How could he let himself be that person in her life when he had twin nephews counting on him for bedtime stories, the right brand of pudding and promises that their mother would come home soon?

As he drove up the drive of the old farmhouse, a shiny new truck pulled in behind him. He parked and the truck parked next to him.

Jason Bradshaw stepped out of the other truck, his grin wide and a pair of work gloves in his hands. Clint met him at the front of his truck, surprised to see the bull rider at his place. Jason, with his strawberry-blond hair and sheepish grin, had lived down the road all of Clint's life, but the younger man had never really been a friend of his.

"Jason, how are you?"

"Better than you." Jason shot a pointed look at Clint's shoulder. "I heard you're going to need surgery. That's a tough break."

"Yeah, but it'll work itself out. What are you up to today?"

"I called up to Willow's and she said you were down here working. I thought I could help."

"You don't have to."

"That's what neighbors do for each other. I just bought the fifty acres next to you. Never know, I might need some help over there someday."

"Okay, then. I guess the first thing I'm going to do is fix that porch."

His phone rang as he was pulling the toolbox out of the back of the truck. He flipped it open, smiling when he heard his sister's voice for the first time in too long. Jason sat down on the tailgate, waiting.

"Sis. How are you?"

A long pause. He wondered if they'd lost their connection. "Jenna?"

"I'm here, sorry, but things are loud. Clint, are the boys okay?"

"Of course they are. They're with Willow, and Janie is taking them to vacation Bible school tonight. They miss you." He heard her sob.

"I miss them, too. But I know if I talk to them, it'll make it worse for them and for me."

"Jenna, is everything okay?"

"Good as it can be."

"And you're eating your vegetables?" He waited for her laughter. This time it was soft, not like her laughter used to be, when she'd been off at college and homesick. That question had always worked on her, a lifetime ago.

"I'm eating my vegetables, but they're dehydrated, and worse than yours. Are the boys eating?"

"Are Oreos a breakfast food?"

"No, Clint, Oreos aren't a breakfast food. Buy them instant oatmeal."

Instant oatmeal. Why hadn't he thought of that? "Okay, I can do that."

"Clint, I have to leave now. I won't be able to call again for a while."

"Why?"

"Gotta run. I love you." And then she was gone and he was holding a phone and he didn't have any way of knowing if she was safe.

"That's tough." Jason held his gloves in his hands and

didn't say more. Clint looked at the other man, wondering about his appearance here, and about the past.

Jason had always been the one smiling, the one joking. And Clint knew his life hadn't been easy. It had just looked easy from the outside.

"Yeah, it's tough," Clint said as he slipped on his gloves. "It's hard to take. I've always been able to protect her."

"Yeah, I know."

"Really?"

Jason Bradshaw, whose smile was as famous as his bull riding, shrugged. But he didn't smile. "She used to sneak out to meet me. I guess you didn't know that."

Clint's fist drew back, and Jason raised a hand, stopping him. "We didn't do anything, Clint. I never did more than hold her hand."

"But she snuck out to meet you?" Anger still simmered as he waited for an explanation.

Jason slipped on the leather work gloves. "Clint, life isn't always pretty, and it's good to have friends who understand and who listen. We were never in love. We were just friends, and we talked."

Clint backed away, no longer wanting to hit the guy. He knew how it felt, to need a friend. Willow flashed to the front of his mind, a friend. Just a friend.

"Well, let's get to work." Jason carried the toolbox.

Clint followed, still thinking about his sister, and about misconceptions. He needed more of an explanation from Jason. "When did the two of you meet?"

"At the hospital—years ago. She was there to see

a friend. I was there—" he didn't look at Clint "—to see my mom."

"I'm sorry, I heard she passed away."

"She'd been sick a long time."

"It couldn't have been easy."

Jason smiled. "No, it was never easy." He set the toolbox on the porch. "After meeting Jenna, and realizing we lived pretty close to each other, we started talking. She was only seventeen, and I knew we weren't going to date, but she was a good friend. We'd sit down there—" he pointed to a tree at the edge of the property, near the pond "—and talk for hours."

"And I thought she had mono, because she was tired all the time." Clint laughed and let it go.

It wasn't as easy to let go of the phone call with Jenna. Pounding nails into wood helped.

Jason Bradshaw handed him more nails, smiling like everything was okay. They were doing all the right things, making life as normal as possible. They were rebuilding a house, and he was taking the boys to vacation Bible school. Normal things that filled normal summer days.

But Jenna was thousands of miles away in Iraq, and her boys were with him. And on top of that, nothing had prepared Clint for the way Willow Michaels would change his life.

It took him by surprise, the need to see her, to talk to her. It had happened a lot lately, that she was the person he thought about when he needed a friend.

At that event in Tulsa, when Janie had reintroduced

them, he'd been afraid that Willow would be one of those people he felt a need to fix. And she wasn't. Maybe he was the one in need.

Bell jumped up from where she'd been sleeping next to the dining room table. She'd crawled into the spot before the boys left with Janie for vacation Bible school. Willow thought that it was because the boys dropped a lot of food when they ate and so Bell received limitless treats off the floor.

Now Bell was jumping and turning in circles, her own way of alerting Willow to a visitor. Willow finished washing the last of the pans from dinner and followed the dog to the door. She watched as Clint's truck pulled to a stop and he got out. He held his left arm to his side, releasing it when he saw her watching. He rolled his shoulders a few times, and then headed for the house, moving slowly.

Willow opened the door and met him on the porch. He carried a plastic bag from the store. From the look on his face, he'd had a long day. He looked haggard, and his shirt was stained. Dust coated his jeans. She motioned him inside.

"Did you get a lot done?" She sat next to him as he struggled to get his boots unlaced.

"Let me." She leaned and untied the laces and then pulled his boots off. When she looked up, he was leaning against the back of the bench, his eyes closed.

"Jenna called," he whispered, not opening his eyes.

"And?"

"She had to go and said she couldn't call for a while. I tried e-mailing her and didn't get an answer."

"There's a logical explanation. She had work to do and just wanted to touch base."

"That's what I've been trying to tell myself all day, but it doesn't feel right. Her conversation didn't feel right."

"You have every right to be worried, Clint."

He opened his eyes. His smile was soft, concerned, tired.

Willow reached, wanting to touch him, but knowing it was the wrong move at the wrong time. They were alone and both lonely. She could see it reflected in his eyes, that he needed to be near someone in the same way she did.

"I have this huge thing of chocolate–peanut butter ice cream." He held up the bag from the local ice cream parlor. "I thought we could share it."

"You just *happen* to have ice cream?"

"I might have driven into town just to buy it, maybe to tempt you into spending time with me."

"It worked." She stood, and then she reached for his hand and pulled him to his feet. They were standing face-to-face, and the room suddenly seemed too small and too warm. "I'll get the bowls."

"I'll help."

He followed her into the kitchen, helping by being in the way each time she turned around. She slid past him to the fridge where she had a nearly full jar of fudge topping. She lifted it, and he nodded.

"We can sit on the porch." He dug a spoon out of the drawer after she twisted the top off the fudge. "It's cool, like it might rain."

"It isn't going to rain, but the porch would be nice." She wanted to say something about the worried look in his eyes. She wanted to tell him that she'd sat on the porch after dinner, and she couldn't hear the crickets.

Instead she handed him a bowl of ice cream and led the way outside. They sat down side by side on the porch swing.

"I wish I could do something to help." She glanced sideways, and he nodded, but he didn't answer.

"Good ice cream," he finally said. But she couldn't tell that he'd even taken a bite.

He leaned back in the seat and stared off into the night. The sun had set, and the security light flickered on. His face was in shadows, smooth planes and stubble on his cheeks. His chest heaved, and she felt, but didn't hear, his sigh.

Willow set her bowl down and reached for his hand, his fingers warm and strong. "I'm praying for Jenna, and for you. I know this isn't easy. But Clint, you're doing a great job with the boys. And Jenna is going to come home real soon and be their mom again."

"Thanks, Willow." He squeezed her hand and smiled. "You've been a big help with the boys. I would have burned more than breakfast if you hadn't showed up when you did."

"I was happy to help."

"You'll be a great mom someday." He smiled, like

the compliment meant everything, and he didn't know how much it hurt.

She looked away, not wanting to deal with his words, an innocent statement that shouldn't have hurt so much, not after so many years. Clint leaned forward, his hand still holding hers.

"Willow, are you okay?"

She turned, trying to smile, trying not to cry. "I'm fine."

"No, you're not." He stroked her fingers. "I'm not sure what I said…"

She couldn't stop the tears or the flash of memories that flickered through her mind. She couldn't stop the images of the accident, and the memory of the pain that followed.

"Willow?" He pulled her close, and she couldn't stop the tears, the aching emptiness that shouldn't still hurt so much.

She would never be anyone's mom. She shook her head, trying to clear her thoughts, trying to undo the moment.

"Willow, I'm sorry." He held her tight, his hands on her back. "Tell me what's wrong."

Tell Clint. Let him into her life, and take the chance that someday this decision to share would bring more pain. More pain and someone else walking away.

He was holding her close. And he had never walked away from her in embarrassment. He had used sign language for a Sunday sermon on peace.

"Clint, I can't have children." She whispered the

words into his neck. He hugged her closer, and his hands stroked her hair.

"I'm sorry." And this time she knew he was sorry because she couldn't have children, not because he'd said the wrong thing.

And she was sorry, too.

She had wanted to hold her baby girl, to give her a name, to raise her and love her. And now, because of one moment, one missed traffic signal, a car horn she hadn't heard, she would never have children.

"Do you want to talk?" He pulled back a little to ask the question and she shook her head, because she wasn't ready to talk. She wanted to stay in his arms for a few more minutes, before realization hit and he put it all together.

She couldn't have children. She would never go through the normal process of falling in love, getting married and having babies.

Her husband had walked away from her the day after their daughter was buried. She couldn't tell Clint, because she didn't want his pity. She didn't want to watch another man walk away.

She brushed away the last remnants of her grief, the tears that still trickled out. She had really thought she'd cried her last. But sometimes the grief sneaked up on her, taking her by surprise. And then came the guilt. It ached deep down inside her heart, where God was still helping her to forgive herself.

Clint was waiting for an explanation. After all of those tears, he deserved one.

"I had a car accident when I was six months pregnant." She rubbed a hand over her eyes and tried to piece it all together again for the man who had held her while she cried. His shirt was still damp from her tears. "When I woke up, my baby was gone, so was my ability to have children, and my marriage was over."

His eyes closed, and she wondered about his thoughts. She remembered Brad closing his eyes, and then opening them, lashing out in anger and blaming the accident on her hearing. When Clint's eyes opened she saw that he was sharing her grief, not condemning her.

Her own emotions did something they rarely did; they took her by surprise. She had a sudden need to keep him in her life, to hold on to his friendship.

I'M SORRY, he signed. That one gesture had never meant so much.

Clint reached for Willow's hand and held it for a long time, not knowing what to say. He knew he couldn't take away her pain. He didn't think she was asking that of him. She had shared because…because why?

A weak moment? Or because they were friends? In that moment it felt like more than friendship. It felt like something he had never experienced. It took him back to that moment when Jenna had called, and he could think only of seeing Willow, talking to Willow.

She was strong. He had never met a stronger woman. He thought of her losing her child, and her husband. He thought of her that day at the doctor's office, stoic, facing whatever was in store for her.

He thought of her prayers for him, for Jenna and for two little boys that missed their mom.

"You're strong, Willow, stronger than you think."

"It's an illusion. At any moment, I could lose it. I could be weak."

"We're all weak at some time or other."

"Maybe so." She stood, gathering their bowls and not speaking further.

"You're okay?" He stood next to her, trying to figure out the next step in this process, and not sure if he should take another step.

"I'm fine." She smiled to prove it. "And you're strong, too."

She kissed his cheek. He had to be strong, because he wanted to pull her against him and make promises he probably couldn't keep. He wanted to kiss her senseless.

He had to leave. He backed away from her, taking the scent of her with him, and remembering the taste of strawberry lip gloss.

She had shared her heartache with him. Now wasn't the time to share other emotions, or ask her if he was imagining something between them that might not exist.

Now wasn't the time. Maybe there wouldn't be a time, because he could see in her eyes that fear of being hurt again.

"I'll see you in the morning." He took another step back. "Do you want me to help you do the dishes?"

She held up the two bowls and smiled, like she

knew that he was stalling. "Two bowls, Clint. I think I can manage."

He nodded. "Okay, I'll go then."

"Don't forget, the boys are spending the night with us."

"Of course." And it was time for him to go. He backed off the porch, holding the rail and smiling as he turned to leave.

"See you tomorrow?" she called out after him.

He turned at his truck, surprised to see her still standing on the porch, and looking like a girl who really did want to know if the guy was coming back.

"Of course."

## *Chapter Ten*

Clint followed Willow out of the house after lunch the next day. The boys were still with Janie, because after a night of movies and popcorn, they weren't ready for the fun to end. Willow was nearly to the barn when he caught up to her. A hand on her arm, and she turned.

"I'm going to visit my dad, and I'm going to pick up a few things for our next trip. Did you need anything in town, or do you want to ride along?"

"Trip?"

"Austin?" Bull riding, like she didn't know what he meant.

"Yes, I know what Austin is. You're not riding."

"I am riding because this is the last event before the summer break. I know that I need surgery. I also know that I can ride. I've been on a few practice bulls."

She shook her head. "You could do more damage."

"I could, but I don't plan on letting that happen. Do you need anything from town?"

"Oh, so you can tell me what to do, but if I try to say anything about your riding, you change the subject."

He pushed his hat down on his head and dug his heels into the firm dirt, and reality. Willow was staring at him, waiting for a response, and he didn't have one. He smiled, because she looked about fit to be tied.

"I'll see you later, Willow."

"I'm going with you."

"Really?"

"You offered." She shifted on booted feet and bit down on her bottom lip. "I do have a few things I could pick up at the store."

"You don't mind running by the nursing home with me?" Willow, going with him, to see his dad. What kind of move into his life was that?

"I don't mind at all."

But did he mind her going? A long time ago, but not that long ago, he'd been a lanky teen with dirty jeans, and girls like Willow wouldn't have climbed into his truck if his had been the last truck out of a burning town. That kid was still inside him, still fighting acne, and dreaming about someday having a wife and a family, maybe a ranch with some cattle and a nice truck.

He hadn't had a lot of time for fun back then, not with farm work, his dad drunk most of the time and Jenna relying on him. He still had that list of priorities, things that had to come first, had to come ahead of his own dreams.

Willow had shifted everything, and now he had to figure out where to put her in his life.

"Where to first?" Willow was talking to him as she pulled her hair back and tied it with a thin scarf. Strawberry lip gloss tinted her lips, and he was having the hardest time of his life remembering his responsibilities.

"The nursing home." He opened the passenger door of his truck for her, and she climbed up, reaching to pull the door closed. He shut it from the outside and took his time getting to the driver's side.

"Why are you acting like I've invaded your personal space?" Willow spoke as soon as he climbed into his truck. "You've been invading *my* space since the day I met you."

He reached to turn down the radio. He didn't need a country song about a stupid boy. Not even if that's what he thought about her ex-husband walking out on her.

"You're not invading my space. I have a lot on my mind."

She was on his mind. Great, all of his thoughts were starting to sound like a country song. If this day ended with the dog getting run over or someone going to prison, he'd switch to rock music.

Intent on letting the conversation drop, he reached to turn up the radio. She turned it up more, smiling. "I like this song."

Of course she did.

They were a mile from the nursing home. "Willow, I need to warn you about my dad."

"Okay."

"He's hard to handle. Sometimes he's in the past, sometimes not. And he says things, sometimes hard things."

"I can handle it."

He knew she could, but he didn't want her to be on the receiving end of one of his father's verbal assaults. "Maybe you should…"

"Wait in the car?"

"I'm sorry."

"If you want me to wait in the car, I will. I'd rather go in with you."

He pulled into the parking lot of the nursing home. "No, I don't want you to wait."

He'd always been the one who was there for others. He'd been there for his dad, and for his sister. Other than Janie, he'd never really thought about having someone "there" for him. But that's what this was about. It was about Willow trying to be there for him. It felt like a new pair of boots, not quite right.

He had put her in the category of another woman he was drawn to who probably needed to be fixed in some way. That had been his track record in the past.

He parked, and she got out of the truck. Willow, tall and beautiful, from a world far removed from his. And she was the one who was going to be there for him as he faced a father who was sinking into a world they couldn't understand.

Her hand slipped into his, and the earlier discussion about riding bulls and being in each other's space faded from his mind. It was no longer important.

At the front desk they signed in as visitors. Willow signed her name next to his. As they walked down the hall, their shoulders brushed, and his hand touched hers. He felt her fingers on his, but they didn't clasp hands. He didn't explain to her about his dad, and about the times the older Cameron had gotten drunk and hit his children because he'd been positive their mother died in that car accident because of them, because she'd been on her way to school to pick them up.

Clint inhaled deeply at the memory of the patrol car pulling up at the school and the social worker helping them into the vehicle.

Willow's fingers slid through his. She knew how his mother had died. She'd explained that Janie told her and she was sorry.

"How long has he been here?"

"A few months. I moved him in here before I moved home."

"That couldn't have been easy. I'm sorry."

She had lost a child and her husband had walked out on her. He kissed the side of her head, his lips brushing her hair. "Thank you."

"Is that you, Clint?" The raspy voice from inside the room carried into the hall.

"It's me, Dad."

"Is Jenna with you?"

Clint led Willow into the room, felt her hesitate at the door, but then she stepped close to his side again.

"No, it's my friend, Willow."

"Where's Jenna?"

Clint sat on the edge of the bed, next to the frail form of his dad. Willow walked to the window. He wondered if the broken-down tractor was still in the field out there and if she was wondering why the farmer had left it that way.

"Dad, Jenna's in Iraq. Remember?"

"Why's the judge's daughter with you?" His dad made a noise in his throat. "You know she's out of your league."

Out of his league. He brushed off old insecurities.

"She isn't the judge's daughter. Willow is Janie's niece."

"The one that can't hear? What's she doing here?"

"Dad, she can hear." He shot Willow an apologetic look, but she was smiling, not at all upset.

"I don't care if she can. Get me some oatmeal that isn't runny. They always bring me runny oatmeal."

"I'll bring some oatmeal later." He poured water instead. "Dad, I'm going to be gone a few days. We're going to Austin."

"Eloping?"

"No, we're going to a bull ride."

"Does she have money? That aunt of hers has money."

"Now you're embarrassing me. And I have my own money."

"Then maybe you ought to get me out of this roach motel."

Willow's laughter was soft, and Clint's dad looked at her. He smiled.

"Dad, when I get home, I'll take you to dinner. How does that sound? Maybe we could go to church together."

"You aren't going to take me to church. I don't have any use for religious people."

And that hurt. Clint couldn't think about this part of his father's life, the part without faith. He closed his eyes, repeating a prayer that he'd repeated numerous times over the years. He wanted his dad to have faith.

"Dad, when I get back, we'll go to church and then we'll go to lunch. We'll get a good steak." Steak for church.

"Fine, we'll go to church if you'll buy me steak. Don't bring those boys or that old woman."

"We'll all go together." He leaned and kissed his dad's thinning gray hair. "We'll go together, Dad. I'll see you next week."

"Goodbye, Mr. Cameron." Willow touched his father's arm as she walked by his bed. "I'll see you at church."

Clint waited at the door for her, and they walked out together. His dad yelled something about not wanting them to elope.

"I'm sorry about that. I did try to warn you."

Willow laughed, soft and easy. "He's something else."

"He's always been something else. He was charming, funny, drunk and mean. The best of all worlds."

"It had to be hard on you, and on Jenna."

"It wasn't easy, but we survived." He pushed the door open and held it for her. "As a teenager life was about faith and surviving, about believing that God really would deliver us from that situation. And as hard as it was, I loved him, and I still love him. He taught me to ride. He taught me to fish. He had his moments."

"Janie said you were a hard worker and everyone loved you."

He grinned, winking as he opened the truck door for her. "Yeah, everyone loved me."

Everyone really did love Clint. Willow watched him walk through the small grocery store in Grove, being greeted by older women and people closer to his own age. Willow walked along behind him, pushing the cart and tossing in items that weren't really on her list. Clint paused at the end of the aisle, talking to a woman with a beehive hairdo and cotton dress. He motioned Willow forward.

"Do you know Janie's niece, Willow Michaels?" he asked the woman, who was giving Willow a look that clearly measured her against Clint and drew a lot of conclusions.

"I don't believe I've met her." The woman smiled.

"Willow, this is Addie Johns. She was my high-school math teacher." He laughed an easy laugh. "And she somehow taught me calculus."

"It wasn't easy." Addie Johns shook her head. "The boy had horses and cows on the brain. And girls."

Clint flushed a light shade of red. "Now, Addie, you know that isn't true."

The older woman laughed and patted his hand. "No, it wasn't true, was it. As a matter of fact, I don't think I've seen you in love before."

Willow choked because Addie Johns meant only one thing by that statement. She was putting them together as a couple. And that couldn't happen.

"Oh, Miss Johns, we're not…"

"Ready to tell everyone." Clint finished Willow's objection and then reached for her hand. "We can trust you to keep it a secret, though."

"Oh, of course." Addie Johns grabbed her cart. "Well, I should get my shopping done. You two have a wonderful day. And don't forget to send me an invitation."

Willow waited until the lady disappeared before punching Clint on the arm. "Why did you do that?"

"To see who would be more surprised, you or Addie. I think you win."

"She'll tell everyone in town."

"More like the entire county." He laughed. "I can hear it now. Phones ringing up and down the line, ladies at home, washing dishes and speculating on a wedding date, and if we'll last, or…"

"Stop." Willow pushed the cart away from him, tossing a few packages of cookies in with a bag of Reese's.

"I was joking, Willow."

"I don't want to be a joke."

He pulled the cart to a stop and stepped close to her side. Willow backed away, feeling the cold of the frozen-food coolers behind her. Clint leaned in, smiling, his gum cinnamon and his cologne a soft hint of pine.

She glared, hoping to put him in his place.

"Okay, it wasn't a joke."

She looked away, even more confused. "Clint, stop."

"Make up your mind, Willow. Do I stop, or do we take a few steps forward to see how this works out?"

Everyone loved Clint. Willow couldn't let herself think those thoughts, or how it felt when he cared about her. He didn't understand the difficulties a relationship with her would include.

"Clint, I have so many things going on in my life right now."

"So do I."

"So, we don't have time for this conversation. Not now. Not here."

"When *do* we have time?" He smiled at a lady pushing her cart past them, a baby in the seat.

"Clint, I can't have children." Her voice broke as she whispered what he already knew, but he hadn't realized that it meant something more.

He was looking at the baby, waving, and Willow was looking at him. Her words registered, and he remembered last night, when he'd held her and it had felt like her heart was breaking, and that a breaking heart was familiar ground to her.

"I know, Willow."

"I can't have children. I can't have a marriage with children." She looked away, but not before he saw the broken look in her eyes.

"You have something that does come with a relationship. Yourself. Willow, when a man falls in love with you, it is about loving *you*."

"What man doesn't want a child with his name, his eyes, his pitching arm or whatever it is that's important to men."

"You're right, I guess, that's something a man does think about. But…"

She reached for the cart. "I can't talk about this."

"You're running from what we both know isn't going to go away." He walked next to her as she headed for the check-out with a cart full of junk food.

Would his feelings for her go away? He wanted to fold her in his arms and hold her forever. He'd never felt that before, not once in his life. It had nothing to do with fixing her.

"There are a lot of things that aren't going away, Clint."

He didn't have a clue what she meant by that, but she was piling groceries on the belt and talking to the cashier. He sighed, because he knew this wasn't the time or place. What had started as a little teasing had gone way wrong.

"Okay, we'll play this your way, Willow. We'll talk later."

She nodded, but he wasn't sure if she heard. And he wondered if later would ever come around.

* * *

Willow sat in her office, thinking about the previous day with Clint—visiting his father, and then the incident at the store. Heat crawled up her cheeks when she thought about Addie Johns calling friends to inform them that Clint had finally found a woman.

Those women had probably been praying for years that Clint would find a nice girl, settle down and have a few kids. Willow finished her candy bar and tossed the wrapper in the trash can.

Why *hadn't* he found a nice girl and gotten married? She thought she'd ask him. Maybe it had to do with chasing his dreams of being a bull rider, and having family obligations.

The phone rang, and she ignored it. She wasn't in the mood to deal with calls or not being able to hear the caller. She buried her face in her hands and waited until the ringing stopped and the answering machine picked up. The words were fuzzy.

Fuzzier than last week. Even fuzzier than a month ago. And she hadn't returned the call to her doctor because she didn't want to know the test results. Not yet. She didn't want to tell Janie, who was busy making arrangements for a trip to Florida with her friends.

She didn't want to tell Clint, because it felt good to have him in her life, treating her like someone who could take care of herself.

The door to her office opened, and Clint peeked in, smiling as he knocked on the side of the door frame.

The boys jumped in ahead of him. They were wearing shorts, T-shirts and rubber boots.

"What are you guys up to?"

"Going fishing." Timmy held up his fishing pool. "Wanna come with us?"

David smiled, his fishing pole held tight in his fist. But he wasn't asking her to go. This morning he had told her he really just wanted his mom's hugs.

"Where are you going fishing?" she asked, looking up to meet Clint's questioning gaze.

"The creek, down by the church." He wore bright-red swim trunks and canvas sneakers. "Come on, be a sport."

"A sport?"

"Yep, the opposite of 'not a sport.' As in, we really want you to come with us."

Timmy shook his head. "We think you have the best snacks."

"Oh, so you have ulterior motives for inviting me?"

"To get you out of this dusty office." Timmy did a deep-voiced imitation of Clint, and Willow laughed.

"Okay, I'll come along. And I'll bring good snacks. We wouldn't want Uncle Clint to burn the house down."

Clint ruffled Timmy's hair. "Good job, buddy. Now you guys run down to the house and get that white cooler for drinks."

Willow watched the boys leave and then she stood, walking around to the front of the desk. Clint was still watching the empty door.

"You okay?" She touched his arm and he turned, his smile a halfway attempt.

"I'm not great. I'm pretty sure I'm failing at this whole guardian thing. David is throwing fits, and Timmy is trying to take over as the 'head of the house.'"

"You're doing fine, Clint. They're just sad little guys right now, and you all have a lot of adjusting to do."

"I guess so, but I sure hope I don't mess them up before she gets back."

"You won't mess them up. I won't let you."

He smiled, and then his expression softened. He touched her hair, and she shivered as his fingers slid down the strand, twirling it around and then letting it drop.

When had she stopped telling him that they couldn't do this, couldn't cross the line? When had his presence in her life started to feel like a forever-dream again?

When would the bottom drop out and leave her heart broken again?

"Having you here was pretty good planning on God's part." He glanced at the door and stepped away from her.

The boys rushed back into the room.

"Ready to go?" Clint asked, like nothing had happened. And Willow decided that nothing had, not really.

Except that Timmy was laughing, and David looked suspicious. Timmy spoke up. "Were you gonna kiss her, Uncle Clint?"

"Now, Timmy, what gentleman asks a question like that?"

"I just wanted to know." The boy dragged his feet a little and looked up, kind of sheepish. Willow didn't buy it because she saw the mischievous glint in his eyes.

"Right." Clint took the cooler. "Come on, let's get good snacks and go fishing."

"I need to check on one of my bulls." Willow grabbed her keys off the desk. "Can I meet you at the house?"

"Do you want me to do something?"

"No, I can do it." She followed them out of the barn, and as they headed across the gravel road to the house, she walked down the side of the fence and climbed over at the padlocked gate.

Dolly had been bullying a younger bull earlier in the day. She wanted to make sure the bigger animal hadn't done any damage. First she had to find him. She saw Dolly. He was standing at the watering trough, looking innocent. The other bull wasn't in sight.

## Chapter Eleven

Clint turned when he heard a bull bellow. He shouted, but Willow didn't turn. She kept walking, as if she had no idea. He yelled again, and the boys screamed. The black bull that had been standing along the far fence was running toward her as she walked in the opposite direction.

"Willow!"

He left the boys standing in the yard and ran. He knew he wouldn't make it in time. He could only pray that he made it in time to keep the bull from killing her. He prayed she would hear him and turn around.

The bull hit her from behind, pushing her to the ground and wallowing her into the dirt. She did what a bull rider would do, curled into a ball and tried to roll out from under the pounding hooves.

Clint climbed the fence and jumped to the ground, yelling at the bull and waving his arms. Willow lay motionless on the ground. The bull changed directions as Bell came running across the field. The dog charged at the bull's legs, leading the animal away.

"Willow?" He dropped to his knees next to her, brushing a hand across her face. "Willow, wake up."

Her eyes opened briefly and then closed again. Clint pulled her close and stood up, holding her limp form in his arms.

"Honey, you sure aren't light." He kissed her forehead. Her eyes fluttered again. "Wake up, okay?"

She blinked again and groaned, her hand going to her head. He watched, helplessly, as blood oozed from the cut. When he was almost to the truck, he shouted for Timmy to open the door.

David stood to the side, his teeth worrying his lip and his eyes wide in fear. He smiled at the boy, hoping to ease his fears.

"She's okay, guys." He prayed he wasn't lying. He slid her into the truck and then rummaged for napkins he'd stored in the console between the seats. "Climb in the back."

He turned and the boys were scurrying to the driver's side to do what he'd asked. He held the napkins to her forehead, and she moaned and opened her eyes again.

"Hold on, we're going to the hospital."

She didn't say anything, and her eyes closed.

Silence and cold were the two things she noticed first. But a warm hand touched her cheek. Willow blinked, and it hurt. Her head ached, and the light hit right behind her eyes. She blinked again and then managed to keep her eyes open. Clint stood in front of her, his expression full of concern.

WELCOME BACK, he signed, his lips moving. No sound.

What had happened? Panic hit, she moved, trying to get up. Pain shot through her head and down her back. She groaned and let firm hands push her back to the mattress.

The nurse smiled, her lips moved. "Calm down."

Willow closed her eyes, trying to remember. She opened them again when Clint's hand touched her arm. His hand, because it was rough, strong, and warm. A doctor stood next to him, asking questions.

DO YOU REMEMBER WHAT DAY IT IS? Clint signed.

"Thursday." She moved her hand to her ears. "Where are the hearing aids?"

BROKEN. DO YOU REMEMBER WHAT HAPPENED?

"I think a truck got loose and ran over me."

CLOSE, IT WAS A BULL. He was smiling, but the lines around his mouth were tight, and humor didn't light his gray eyes.

"It felt like a truck." She wanted to smile, but everything hurt. And she shuddered, remembering. She remembered the ground vibrating, and being hit from behind. That big head had pushed her down, and her forehead had hit something hard.

YOU REMEMBER WHAT HAPPENED? Clint's hands moved, asking the question.

"Yes, I remember. I think the bull knocked me down. I was going to check on him."

Clint sat down on the stool next to her bed. *Willow, you didn't hear me.*

She looked away, smiling when Janie walked through the door. "I'm fine. I'm not sure why the two of you look so worried."

WE'RE WORRIED BECAUSE WE... He looked away. BECAUSE WE CARE ABOUT YOU.

She touched her head, wincing because the pain was sharp. She hadn't heard Clint. Tears squeezed between closed eyes, warm on her cheeks. She shivered, and a blanket slid over her.

When she opened her eyes, Clint was there, no one else. "Thank you for being here."

"That's what friends do. They help each other. You've helped me with the boys. You've given us a place to stay, and you make them feel safe." He signed the words and his lips moved.

"They're easy to love." She covered his hand that rested on her arm. "Where did Janie go?"

"She left so that I could talk to you."

"Oh." An intervention. Great.

"You didn't hear me."

"Maybe you weren't shouting loud enough."

"Willow, you have to tell us what's going on. We care about you." His hands moved as he spoke, showing his anger in a way that she clearly understood. "I guess you don't have to tell me, but I do think you owe Janie an explanation."

She looked away, not ready for this, for finding out the truth about his friendship. Would it last when he learned the truth? He touched her arm, and she couldn't ignore him, or the truth, any longer.

And she reminded herself how few hearing people had ever taken the time to sign for her. She'd always relied on reading lips. Clint had bridged that gap. He didn't have to.

"I know that I owe you both an explanation. But I didn't want this to keep Janie from moving."

"This."

"My hearing is going to get progressively worse."

EXPLAIN, he signed.

"Profound hearing loss. The hearing aids will be practically or totally useless. It's hard to tell at this point."

He sighed, and his hand went to his chest, his fist circling his heart. I'M SORRY.

She nodded, because what else could he say, or she say? This was it, the truth, the inevitable. This was where she learned how strong a friendship they had.

This is where she found out if he stayed in her life or walked.

"It isn't the end of the world." She'd had a few days to deal with the news. She could see shock all over his face.

"Of course it isn't." He smiled as he said the words.

Reality was easy to think about, until a person was face-to-face with it. Complete hearing loss—a huge change in how she lived, and how the people around her lived their lives.

It changed everything.

"Where are the boys?" she asked.

IN THE WAITING ROOM WITH JANIE, he signed, and she nodded.

"We should go. They're probably hungry. And I ruined their day at the creek."

"The boys are fine with Janie. She's going to take them home, and she's going to call your folks to let them know what happened."

"No, don't call my parents. They'll just worry, and I don't want them to worry."

THEY'RE YOUR PARENTS, Clint signed, and then he stood up, like he meant to leave. She didn't want him to go. "And they'll be hurt if they find out later."

"I have a concussion, and my head hurts. I need to sleep."

NO SLEEPING. A new doctor entered the room, a woman with short brown hair and fingers adept at signing. YOU'LL HAVE TO STAY AWAKE FOR A WHILE. AND I WOULD REALLY LIKE IT IF YOU WOULD SPEND THE NIGHT.

Willow groaned and closed her eyes. "No, please don't make me spend the night."

It felt like five years ago, when everyone made the decisions for her. But it wasn't. This time she had Janie and Clint. And she had faith. Five years ago she had really and truly been on her own, with God as an afterthought, filed somewhere at the back of her mind like so many other childhood memories.

"Does she have to spend the night?" Clint signed and spoke to the doctor, not leaving Willow out of the conversation. "We can keep an eye on her."

The doctor looked from Willow to Clint. "I want

her to stay for a few hours, and then we'll discuss her going home."

Clint patted her arm to get her attention. "I'll go talk to Janie about taking the boys home. Or I can take them home, and Janie can stay with you. Either way, one of us will be here."

Willow closed her eyes and nodded. When she opened them, Clint was gone. He was talking to Janie. Or had he left? She couldn't find a clock on the wall and had no way of knowing what time it was or how long she'd been there. She closed her eyes again, wanting to escape the pain, because it wasn't just the bumps and bruises from the bull that hurt.

Willow was asleep when Clint walked through the curtain partition that separated her from other patients. He didn't want to wake her, but knew he had to. She looked peaceful in sleep, as if it was rest that she needed.

He touched her arm, and her eyes flickered and opened. His smile brought one from her, and then her hand touched the place on her forehead where they'd given her a few stitches.

"Ouch," she whispered. "That's going to leave a mark."

He smiled and laughed a little. "Yes, it's going to leave a mark."

"Does it look bad?"

YOU LOOK BETTER THAN YOU DID, he signed, and then laughed. "Not that you ever look bad. I mean, you usually look great."

"I'm not sure if I feel hurt or complimented." She pushed the button and lifted the bed to a sitting position. "I do know that I'm ready to get out of here."

"You have to stay until the doctor releases you. And I wouldn't push her. She isn't in favor of you leaving today."

"The boys…"

"Are fine with Janie." He scooted the stool closer to her side. "Willow, this is serious. We need to come up with a plan."

"Clint."

He lifted his hands and shook his head. "You're right, none of my business."

"No, it isn't your business." She smiled past him, and he turned in time to see a nurse walk away. Willow's hands began a quick firing of words. I DON'T WANT TO HAVE TO COME UP WITH A PLAN.

WHY?

AVOIDANCE. I KNOW WHAT'S HAPPENING TO MY OWN BODY. I ALSO KNOW THAT IF JANIE KNOWS, SHE'LL PUT OFF MOVING.

YOU THINK YOU'RE ONLY STRONG IF YOU HOLD ON AND DON'T LET PEOPLE HELP YOU.

I'VE LET YOU HELP. She smiled like it all made perfect sense. "Now, I really want to get out of here, Clint. I want to sleep in my own room. I want to have breakfast with Janie and the boys."

"For a price I could see if it could be arranged."

"For a price?"

"You have to let friends face this with you. You're

not alone, so stop acting like you are." He smiled, to soften the words. "Trust your friends."

"I know, and I do trust you. But you have your hands full with the boys. And if this is going to happen, I have to deal with it and learn how to keep going."

"I know, but just remember, you can trust me."

Trust. An easy little word but with so many complications.

It was easy to commit to someone when things were going well, when there were no obstacles in the way. But obstacles could damage any relationship, even something as simple as friendship.

She was going to lose her hearing. End of story. That was a big complication.

Clint touched her hand, drawing her attention back to him. "It's going to be okay. And I'm going to be here to help."

"I know. And I do trust you."

"You're saying what you think I want to hear because you want something. You want to go home."

She shrugged. "Is it working?"

"No."

Of course not. He wasn't easy to dissuade. He wasn't prone to chasing rabbits or getting off track.

"Okay, fine, we'll talk. I've been dealing with this, trying to get through it and adjust."

"But you're doing this alone, and we could have helped."

"You won't always be here." She shifted her gaze toward the window, away from his sympathy. "Janie won't always be here. What am I going to do with my business when I can't hear a caller on the telephone, or announcers at events?"

"I get it." He stood but he didn't move away. "But I don't get why you think you're doing this alone."

"I know that I'm not. I'm just trying to prepare."

"We can help you with that."

She shook her head. "No, you can't. You can't help me face how people will react."

"Which means?"

"There are three different ways people can react. One. Let me keep living my life, and keep treating me the way I've been treated. Second. Some people will walk away, because it's just too difficult to deal with. Or the third option, start treating me like I can't take care of myself."

He nodded, not answering right away. And she wondered which option he would choose.

"One day at a time, Willow. That's how we'll deal with this."

He kept saying "we" like he meant to stay in her life. Each time he said it her heart battled between wanting to believe and being afraid to believe.

"Yes, one day at a time."

I'M NOT GOING ANYWHERE. He signed it with force.

"I know you aren't. Now go see if you can break me out of here. I promise to be good."

He nodded. "I'll see if I can make a deal."

"Thank you."

He walked out the door and after he left she sighed and leaned back against the bed. Clint wanted to make sure she survived whatever might happen to her in the future.

Thirty minutes later he lifted her off her feet and carried her the short distance from the doors of the hospital to his waiting truck. Her arms were around his neck, and when she argued that she could walk, he shook his head.

She'd correctly guessed his type. He was a rescuer. He couldn't help himself. It was as much a part of him as his eye color, as his faith, as his sense of loyalty. And it wasn't a bad thing, his need to rescue.

Maybe he needed rescuing, too? That thought brought a smile that she hid in the soft curve of his shoulder. She could rescue him.

He opened the truck door and leaned in to set her on the seat. His arms were around her, and hers were still wrapped around his neck. His breath, minty and warm, touched her cheek as he drew back, and he paused, his hands resting lightly on her arms.

As they stared at one another, Willow tried to think of something to say. Words failed her. Clint's hand brushed hair back from her face and lingered at the nape of her neck.

"I'm going to kiss you." His hands also signed the words, soft and beautiful, like a whisper.

"We'll regret this tomorrow." The words edged past the tightness in her throat.

"Maybe."

As he leaned closer, Willow held her breath, waiting for that moment when Clint's lips touched hers. It wasn't a fleeting kiss, not a promise of something more to come. The kiss *was* the promise. It felt like forever, warm and firm, touching places forgotten, or places she'd never known.

She slid her hands through his hair and waited for reality to return as his soft curls wrapped around her fingers. The kiss went deeper, and her emotions took flight as his hands rested on her back, holding her close.

A long moment, and they pulled apart. Willow couldn't talk, she nearly couldn't breathe. That kiss had felt different, it had felt dangerously close to falling in love. Clint leaned against the door of the truck, looking like he'd been run over by the same bull that hit her. He pushed a hand through his hair and whistled.

Who was rescuing whom?

"That was either the best thing I've ever done, or the biggest mistake of my life."

Willow's mouth opened and she shook her head. Reading lips could sometimes be a problem. Surely she'd misunderstood. "Big mistake?"

His fingers moved, slow and a little shaky. HOW DO WE GO BACK TO FRIENDSHIP?

Lines drawn and now smudged. Badly smudged. She'd drawn those lines herself, knowing she had to find the place where he fit comfortably into her world, where he wasn't a threat, and where he was least likely to hurt her.

What now?

"I'm not sure, Clint. But I'd like to go home." Because suddenly—maybe because of the head injury, or maybe because of a kiss—she couldn't remember why it had been so important to her that he be only a friend.

And now *he* seemed to think they could only be friends.

He started to say something, and Willow looked away, avoiding his words. He touched her shoulder, and she shook her head. She wasn't going to listen. She signed the words, and he turned her so that they were facing each other.

NOT FAIR, he signed.

"Kissing me like that and calling it a mistake wasn't fair." She lifted her chin a notch, more for confidence than a statement of defiance. "I need time to think, and I really don't want to listen to what you have to say. If I have to, I'll close my eyes."

He laughed. "That's about the most juvenile thing I've ever heard from a grown woman."

"Yes, it is, isn't it? Juvenile, but effective."

She couldn't stay mad at him when she'd been thinking what he'd had the nerve to say. A great kiss, or a big mistake. She thought maybe it fit into both categories.

## Chapter Twelve

Clint left Willow in Janie's capable hands that first night, and the next day she spent resting. Janie insisted. He waited until the second day after the accident to face her again, and to let the boys visit.

The boys had demanded it. A whole day without Willow had been too much for them. He followed them into the house, warning them to take it easy because she might not feel like having company. Especially rowdy four-year-old company.

But he figured his company would be the least welcome, because he had stepped a little too far into her life. As much as it had felt as if she enjoyed being in his arms, as much as he enjoyed having her there, it had definitely done something. It had put distance between them.

Maybe because they both had a lot to think about. He sure hadn't been expecting this when he met her. He hadn't been looking for these feelings.

As he walked down the hall, he heard Janie in the back room, talking to the boys. Willow was silent. He walked into the sitting room where the boys were chattering to Janie, and Willow was trying to follow along. As he walked through the door, he signed their excited words for her.

Willow smiled over their heads, and the boys continued to jabber about the kittens crawling around in the barn and Bell chasing a mouse.

"Guys, get off Willow. Give her a break." He signed as he spoke to the boys, making sure she didn't get left out.

"They're fine. They're just excited about their new trucks."

"They're going to play, and then we're going to try the creek again." He sat down on the couch next to Willow.

"Sounds like fun. I think I'll not go this time."

"You didn't make it last time."

"And because of me, the boys missed out on fishing and the rope swing." She hugged both boys and kissed the tops of their heads. Clint told himself it was silly to be jealous of little boys.

"I think they understood." He pulled the boys to his side and gave them each a bear hug. "I'm going to get some work done this morning. We'll do the creek this afternoon, guys. For now, the two of you can play outside where I can see you."

Willow followed him to the front door. As the boys grabbed their cars and ran off for a dirt patch that they were itching to dig around in, Willow caught hold of his arm.

"Clint, don't do this."

"Do what?"

"Don't treat me different. Don't let my hearing, a kiss, whatever has happened, don't let it change things between us." She bit down on her bottom lip and shrugged, "I don't want to lose your friendship."

"You haven't lost me, Willow."

"Haven't I?"

"No, you haven't. I have a lot on my mind. Yes, I'm worried about you. I'm worried about what this all means to your future here. I'm worried because I haven't had an e-mail from Jenna. I'm worried because the boys miss their mom. I'm about exhausted from worry."

"Then don't let me be one of the things you worry about. I'm fine. I've been taking care of myself for a long time now, and I'm going to keep taking care of myself. I'm not giving up on this farm, or raising bulls. I'll figure something out. And I'm still very capable of helping with the boys. Don't take that away from me."

"I'm sorry, Willow." He brushed a hand through his hair. "This isn't about you. It's me. I'm just tired, and I have work to do in the barn."

"Okay, go work in the barn. I have an appointment in town." She pulled him back. "Hey, that's my barn. Is there something going on that I should know about?"

Well, he really hadn't wanted to deal with this right now. But from the look on her face, he wasn't going to have the chance to walk away without telling her everything.

"Nothing important, just going to clean the stalls and meet James McKinney later. He wants to look at that little cow you were talking about selling, the Hereford."

"James McKinney is coming to look at one of my cows? James doesn't like my cows."

"They're cows like everyone else's."

"No, not in James's mind they're not." She frowned, and it was cute. "I think in his mind my cows are city cows."

"Well, he must have changed his mind. I saw him at the feed store, and he mentioned buying a cow for his granddaughter. She's joined 4-H."

"And you offered to sell him my cow."

"You told me you wanted to sell her." He shook his head. "Willow, I'm just about confused now. If you don't want to sell that heifer, I'll call him and tell him not to come over."

"Go ahead and sell her." She turned and walked back inside the house. Bell sat on the porch staring at Clint and then looking at the door.

"She even has you confused, doesn't she?" He patted his leg, and the dog followed him out to the barn.

After cleaning out a few stalls Clint fixed a bottle for the calf and held it over the fence. The black-and-white animal nudged the bottle and then latched on and drank down the milk in a matter of minutes. Clint pulled the bottle away and dumped grain into the trough.

"That's it, buddy." He dropped the bottle in the bucket, sat it inside the barn and then walked through the dry, dusty lot. He glanced up, hoping for a sign of rain. Not a cloud in the sky. It was near the end of June, and they could use a good soaking before the grass dried up and they had to start hauling in hay from somewhere else.

The cow he was going to show James McKinney was in the corral. He'd brought her up last night, separating her from the rest of the herd to make it easier to show her today. When she saw him coming she mooed a pitiful sound, asking for her companions and some grain. He lifted the bucket of grain he'd carried out for her. That'd have to be enough to keep her happy.

A deep red with brown eyes in a white face, she lumbered to the feed and shoved her nose into the molasses-covered corn and oats, snorting and blowing it across the metal trough. He reached through and rubbed the top of her head. She jerked away, grain slobbering from her mouth as her tongue licked to draw it back in.

"Yeah, you're not the only female mad at me." He lifted his leg and hooked his boot on the lower rail of the fence. "I'm a pretty unpopular guy this morning."

"Talking to yourself, Clint?"

He turned and smiled at Janie. She wore polyester pants, a loose top and rubber work boots. He smiled, remembering her fifteen years before, out in a storm trying to save one of her prize cows, which had been having difficulty giving birth. She'd pulled out the calf that had refused to exit the birth canal, and then she'd pushed on that mama cow until she got to her feet. She had saved them all, including Jenna and him.

"Yeah, I guess I am."

"You're going to have to stop trying to be such a hero." Janie reached through and rubbed her hand along the floppy ear of the cow.

"What do you mean by that?"

"I mean that all of her life Willow has had people making decisions for her. This ranch was the one thing she did on her own. Now, more than ever, she needs to feel like she's still in control."

"I'm helping."

"You *were* helping. But this accident and the test results changed things." Janie's eyes watered. "Oh, Clint, we don't want to think of Willow going through something like this. But she's facing it, and she's determined. Don't treat her any differently."

"I'm not." He sighed. "I sure don't mean to."

"Did you mean to fall in love with her?"

He laughed at that. "Janie, one thing I'm not is in love. I'm here to help Willow for as long as she needs me. But I don't have time for relationships. I've got two little boys to raise and a farm to rebuild."

Janie patted his arm, the way she'd been doing since he was a twelve-year-old kid, asking for odd jobs. "You're a little too convinced you're the only one who can take care of everyone, but you've got a good heart."

"It isn't bad to take care of people that you care

about." The rumble of a truck coming down the drive sounded like an escape.

"No, it isn't bad, unless you are so busy taking care of everyone that you forget to let them into your life." She glanced in the direction of the old, blue farm truck pulling up to the barn. "That's old McKinney. I'm leaving before he can ask me to have coffee at the café."

"Maybe I'm not the only one so busy taking care of everyone that I forget to let people into my life." He shot the comment at her retreating back.

Janie turned, smiling. "I guess you learned it from me. Is that a good thing, Clint?"

He shrugged. "I don't know, Janie. You've always seemed pretty content."

"Think about what I've said. I'm going to check on the boys. They're playing out front. Willow went to get new hearing aids."

"See you in a bit."

She continued on, her boots scuffing in the dusty dirt. Clint sighed and leaned his back against the fence. Janie, in her sixties and alone all of these years. He couldn't remember one time that she ever went out with someone, other than her friends from church.

He wondered if she ever got lonely. And if someday he would look back on his life, a life without someone to share it with, and regret. His entire life he'd spent taking care of Jenna and his dad, and later, the boys. And love had seemed like something that didn't really last.

James McKinney walked through the gate and headed in his direction. The old farmer's eyes were on the cow, and he was nodding. Clint fought back a smile. James McKinney had more money than most banks. He actually owned part of a bank or two. But like so many of the older farmers, you couldn't tell by looking at him. He drove a twenty-year-old truck that he didn't see a need to replace. He lived in a house that hadn't seen a new roof in thirty years and was still being heated with wood and cooled with fans.

James McKinney was the old guard of farming, the guys who didn't go into unnecessary debt and raised cows for meat, not show. He didn't have no use, he would say, in pedigrees. He wanted a cow that would produce good calves.

Until now. And Clint knew that girls changed everything. Even a crusty old farmer.

"She looks good, Clint. Why's Willow getting rid of her?"

"She has to cull a few, James."

"You wouldn't try to pull one over on an old guy, would you, Clint? Your daddy pulled a few good ones on me." The older farmer laughed. "He sold me a horse one time, told me she was a champion of some kind. That horse was nothing but the champion of running her rider through barn doors."

"I remember that horse." Clint smiled. "Sorry about that. And no, I don't deal like my dad did."

"That's good to know." James walked around the cow, looking from all angles. "I hate to even admit this, but my granddaughter wants a cow to show in community fairs."

Clint nodded. He understood. A man would do strange things for a woman. "Well, things change, James. And I bet grandkids change a man even more."

"You wouldn't believe it if I told you." He scratched his chin and nodded, slow, thoughtful. "She looks like a good little heifer. Gentle, too."

"She likes most people." Everyone but him.

"You couldn't get a better heifer for your grand-daughter, James." Willow's voice. She walked toward them, smiling and dismissing Clint with a look. He backed away, because he knew that territorial look on her face. He'd seen barn cats like her, circling their territory, backs arched.

"Will she lead?" James asked Clint. Clint looked at Willow. Nope, she wouldn't lead, and she sure couldn't be pushed.

He wasn't sure what to do, but Willow was looking at him, so he signed the other man's inquiry because the questioning look on her face said she hadn't heard.

"Yes, she'll lead," Willow answered.

James McKinney looked from Willow to Clint, as if he wasn't sure which one of them he should be talking to. Clint pointed to Willow, it was her cow. He was just the unlucky guy that was trying to help.

"Do you think she'd make a show cow?" James McKinney muttered and shook his head as he glanced over the heifer, his back to Willow. Clint signed the question and Willow adjusted the new hearing aids she had obviously gone to Grove to pick up.

"She will, James." Willow had a lead rope, and she

walked through the gate and snapped it onto the halter the cow wore. "Stand aside, gentlemen."

She led the cow out of the pen and closed the gate behind her. She walked up to James McKinney and handed him the corded rope. "Take her home with you, James. I'm sure Clint already gave you a price."

Ouch. But she was right, he had given the farmer a price, the one Willow had quoted him earlier. He pretty much knew at that moment that he was in serious, very serious, trouble.

Willow left Clint with James McKinney and walked across the lawn to the swing where the boys were sitting, the two of them together. They were always together.

She shot a look in the direction of the barn and Clint saying goodbye to James McKinney. Ignoring him was the only way for her to take back her space. She'd lived through this before, with her parents, and with other men.

She had wanted Clint to be different. She had wanted him to not be her dad, with a protective streak and that need to make decisions for her, as if she couldn't. She had hoped he wouldn't be the man that couldn't handle her deafness.

Her heart leaped to his defense. He had signed for her, allowing her to be included in the conversation with James.

She pulled back on the ropes of the swing and gave the boys a little push. They looked back, smiling, but not laughing.

Each week that passed, missing their mother got harder, not easier for them. With her trip to Austin canceled—thanks to her accident—they wouldn't have to travel for a few weeks. They could all use a break and a little stability.

She pushed the boys a little harder, a little higher. They were still quiet, still not themselves. She brought them back to earth, holding tight to the ropes until the swing came to a halt.

"Do you guys want ice cream?" She moved to the front of the swing and squatted in front of them.

They nodded, their little faces dirty and their hair sticking out in all directions. They needed a bath. Men didn't notice those things.

"Hey, I have an idea. Why don't the two of you put on swim trunks, and we'll turn on the hose. You can play in the water, cool off, and I'll even get some soap for you to bubble up with."

They looked on board with her plan until she mentioned soap. But they needed it. She knew they'd been playing in the driveway, making miniature roads through the dirt and gravel for their toy cars.

"Come on, ice cream and a shower in the garden hose." She smiled, making it sound like a great idea.

Timmy finally nodded and slid off the swing, a hand on David's arm pulling the smaller twin along with him. "Come on, David, you're starting to stink."

Willow smiled, because she knew Timmy had heard that from someone. Probably from Clint. The boys ran ahead of her, in a hurry for the ice cream, not the baths.

"You boys need to find swim trunks for the hose."

They were running away from her, and if they answered, she didn't hear them. But they would know where to find what they needed. While they got ready and picked ice cream, she'd drag out the hose.

A shadow near the barn. Clint. He waved and walked back into the shadows. She saw him tug out his cell phone, and then a dark sedan pulled down the drive. Willow stopped to watch, her heart hurting as the men stepped out of the car and walked up to Clint.

The boys were running into the garage where the extra freezer held the boxes of ice cream bars. She followed along at a slower pace. She laughed as she walked into the dark room, but she didn't feel like laughing. The boys were stripping, and under their clothes they had on swim trunks.

"You guys are ready to go?"

"We wanted to go to the creek today," Timmy explained. "Uncle Clint said he'd take us later."

"Okay, grab a fudge bar or ice cream sandwich. Oh, and there are orange Push-Ups."

The two of them were rummaging, looking for their favorites. Willow smiled as she walked out the back door. The hose was on a caddy. She pulled it loose and hooked it to the sprinkler. When the boys walked out, ice cream dripping down their chins, she was ready for them. She turned on the water and pointed.

"There you go. Finish your ice cream and then jump in. I'll get towels and soap."

"No soap!" David looked at her and said the words with a disgusted face that left no room for doubt.

"Sweetie, you have to get clean."

"'Cause you stink." Timmy was nodding, like he was the expert on stinking. "You smell worse than my dirty socks."

Pleasant. Willow wrinkled her nose at them. "Dirty socks is a bad smell, David. I'll be right back."

She glanced at the barn as she walked through the garage. Clint was standing near the barn door, his hat in his hands and his face pointed away from her. The car was gone. The boys were laughing and jumping through the sprinkler. She wanted them to stay young and innocent. She didn't want their hearts to be broken.

## Chapter Thirteen

Clint watched the car drive away and then he looked across the drive to see Willow with the boys. He couldn't go over there, not yet. The boys disappeared around the side of the house, carrying ice cream. Clint smiled at that, at the sight of them being little boys, and Willow being herself with them. He could hear the boys shouting something about cold and then squeals combined with laughter. Willow's laughter melted with theirs.

He wanted to laugh with them, to tell them everything would be okay. But he couldn't. He headed their way. At the corner of the house he stopped and watched. They were running under the cold spray of the sprinkler. They had soap, and they would step out of the water, scrub and run back under the water. A creative way to get them clean. He wanted to smile, and he wanted to cry.

Willow turned, smiling when she saw him. She was

sitting in a lawn chair, blond and perfect, jean shorts and a T-shirt, her hair pulled back. He must have revealed something because her smile dissolved and she stood up. As she crossed the yard, slipping past the boys and the spray from the hose, he prayed for strength.

He prayed that God would do something huge. He prayed his sister would come back home alive.

That she would come back.

His eyes burned and his chest felt tight.

It all looked so normal. It looked like any other day. The boys were playing, splashing on a summer afternoon, with the blue Oklahoma sky a backdrop for their fun, and bees buzzing over the flowers on a nearby bush.

How could it look like everything was okay, when it was anything but?

"Clint?"

He looked up. Willow stood in front of him, nearly as tall as he was. Her blue eyes met his and held his gaze, looking deep, like she could see into his heart. He hoped she couldn't, because the thoughts in there were pretty scrambled right about then.

"I can't talk about it." He touched her shoulder as he passed. He couldn't talk yet. Not because he didn't want to, but because he couldn't get the words past the tight lump in his throat.

"Aunt Janie?" Willow rushed past him, opening the screen door on the back of the house. "Could you come out here and watch the boys?"

Janie walked out, smiling, wiping her hands on a

kitchen towel. She glanced from him to Willow and then to the boys. Her eyes narrowed, and he looked away, not able to tell her, not yet. He needed a few minutes to get it together, for everyone's sake. For the boys' sake.

"Clint?"

He shook his head and walked past her, into the air-conditioned dining room of her house. Willow followed him inside, her hand rested on his shoulder while he gathered his thoughts and fought back the wave of fear that got tangled with faith, as he tried to tell himself God could take care of Jenna.

"She's missing." He whispered the words and then turned and said them again. "Jenna is missing."

"Oh, Clint." Her only words as she stepped close and her arms wrapped around his waist, holding him tight.

One harsh sob escaped the lump in his throat and Willow's tears were hot on his neck. He had to hang on, to be strong. If he looked outside he would see the boys, playing in the mist of the sprinkler. A summer day, blue skies, and people relying on him. For just a few minutes he wanted to not be that person.

"What happened?" Willow whispered against his neck.

He moved back a step and closed his eyes as he took a deep breath. Willow's hand remained on his arm. When he opened his eyes she moved her hand to his cheek and a soft, tremulous smile curved her lips.

"Her unit was moving and it was attacked. They can't find her anywhere."

"They'll find her."

"What if…"

"We're not going to give up, Clint. We're going to keep praying and keep having faith."

"I know. I know." But his heart ached and faith was in short supply at the moment.

"I'm going to pray, Clint. I'm going to have enough faith for both of us right now."

He closed his eyes and breathed in, nodding his agreement. Right now that's what he needed.

He glanced out the window and saw Janie with his nephews. The boys needed him. As much as he wanted to stay in Willow's arms, he knew that his priority was outside, with two little boys who were about to learn that their mother was missing.

"Don't tell them." Willow grabbed his arm. "Not yet, Clint. Give the military time to find her. Give the boys this day to play."

Before he took away their sunshine.

How would they recover from this? Would they? He brushed a hand through his hair and watched as the boys played, splashing fine mists of water at Janie. She raised the towel and laughed. But he could see that her laughter was strained, because she knew.

As he watched, Janie looked his way, her smile fading. Willow's hand still held his arm, like she thought her hold on him would keep the inevitable from happening.

"I have to tell them. I can't keep this from them."

"They're babies."

He sighed, wishing the huge breath he took would relieve the tightness in his chest. It didn't. The truth was still there, heavy on his heart. He smiled down at Willow. Her gaze had left his face, and she was looking out the window, at his nephews. He lifted the hand she'd placed on his arm and kissed her palm.

Her gaze shifted back to his face. "Don't tell them, Clint. Don't make them carry this weight. We can carry it for them until we know something definite."

*Definite.* The word hit like an arrow. Until he knew for sure if his sister was coming back to them. He held on to Willow's hand, knowing she would let go of her anger with him for this time, while he needed her.

And he did need her.

He'd never needed anyone before, not the way he needed her. All of his life he'd taken care of things, of people, and he'd been just fine with that.

He couldn't even think about when it had started, this needing her. And now more than ever, the boys needed him. They needed him strong.

"You're right. We won't tell them. Not yet."

She nodded and walked out the door ahead of him, already wearing a smile for the boys to see. But he had seen the look in her eyes before she turned away. Her eyes reflected her sorrow, for him, for the boys and for Jenna.

He pasted on a smile of his own as he walked out to join the boys under the sprinkler, not caring that his clothes got soaked.

Life had just taken a sudden turn, and now, everything

was about Timmy and David and getting through the days and weeks to come. His gaze connected with Willow's. She stood just at the edge of the spray of water, letting it hit her arms and face. He could see the tears still trickling out of her eyes as she watched the boys play.

The boys wouldn't let him remain in his stupor. Timmy splashed him, and when Clint smiled, the child stood for a moment studying him. Like he knew something was wrong. Clint forced a bigger smile and splashed back.

"Why don't you guys finish up and we'll go back to our house for a little while. You can put on dry clothes, and then we'll cook hot dogs."

"Could we make a fire?" David edged out of the water and his thumb went to his mouth.

"We can build a fire, yes."

"Do you have marshmallows?" Timmy stood under the spray of water, and he still didn't look convinced that everything was okay.

"I don't have marshmallows."

"We have some," Janie offered.

Clint backed out of the water, still unable to really make eye contact with Janie or Willow. "Thanks. The two of you can join us."

"I can't tonight, Clint." Janie pushed herself out of the lawn chair she'd been sitting in. "Willow can come down. We have all of the fixings for s'mores."

Timmy grabbed Willow's hand. She looked at Clint, and he knew she'd lost part of the conversation.

He signed the plan for her. She smiled down at Timmy and nodded. "I'll be down, sweetie. We can sing and make s'mores. It'll be fun."

Timmy and David, soaked and shivering from the cold well water, grabbed his hands.

"Let's go." Timmy pulled on him, and Clint smiled goodbye to Willow and Janie.

At six-thirty Willow walked down the drive to the foreman's house. Clint was at the edge of the drive, making a circle with rocks for the fire. The garden hose was out, because the grass was dry for so early in the summer. Willow smiled because the boys were dragging huge limbs they'd found at the edge of the yard to the fire pit.

Timmy walked backwards, pulling on a limb that had to be ten feet long. David dropped his and brushed his hands off on his denim shorts. He picked it up again and heaved to set it in motion. An offer to help would have crushed him, so she watched, praying he wouldn't get hurt.

"They're having fun." Clint spoke when she was close. He placed the last rock and sat back on his heels.

"They're definitely having fun." She pulled up one of the lawn chairs he had set out and lowered herself, still aching from the run-in with the bull.

"You okay?" Clint stood, dusting his hands off on his jeans and then pulling up a chair for himself.

"I'm good. It's you I'm worried about. And the boys."

WE'LL GET THROUGH THIS, he signed, AND JENNA WILL COME HOME.

SHE WILL, CLINT. I KNOW SHE WILL, she signed back, rather than speaking. This protected the boys from overhearing. She didn't want them to hear this conversation.

He nodded and glanced in the direction of the boys. They were still dragging too-large limbs, huffing and puffing as they made their way across the yard. "I should help them."

"They're fine. But we should probably find some smaller pieces of wood."

He grinned at that. "You're a campfire girl?"

"I happen to know a few things about camping." She stood up and reached for his hand. "Come on, let's help the boys."

YOU'RE HELPING ME, WILLOW. He spoke the words with his hands, and she silently thanked God for good friends. "Thank you for coming down here tonight."

"I wouldn't have left you on your own."

"Yes, you would have."

"No, Clint, I wouldn't have. This is no longer about us. It's about two little boys." She lifted his hand and kissed his knuckles. "It's about you, too. Friends help each other."

As they crossed the yard to trees at the back of the house, Clint didn't comment.

"Janie talked to our pastor." Willow reached for a few twigs for kindling. "He wants to have a prayer service tomorrow night."

"What about the boys?"

"We'll take them to the nursery and let them play."

"Okay." He touched her arm and pointed back to the house. "They want to eat."

Willow turned and smiled at the boys. They were standing at the corner of the house, side by side.

"I think we're being summoned." Clint grabbed a few more small limbs. "Coming, guys."

Willow followed Clint back to the front of the house and dumped her wood next to the pile the boys had dragged up. With that amount of wood, they'd have a fire until late into the night. And maybe that's what Timmy and David planned.

She sat down in the lawn chair and watched as Clint piled kindling and paper. He struck a match, and a little flame burst into life, catching the paper and the smallest twigs.

And then it went out.

He tried again. Willow snickered and the boys laughed. Clint gave her a look and shook his head, but his lips turned into a little smile. A sheepish smile that flickered and then dissolved as he bent to concentrate on the fire, and worry. She knew he was worried.

"I can do this." He struck another match.

"Of course you can." Willow agreed, but she shook her head, and the boys laughed again.

Clint sat back on his heels and tossed her the matches. "Go ahead, smarty pants, you get it started."

Willow stood. "Okay, I'll make you a deal. I'll get the fire started, and you have to roast my hot dogs."

"Done." He held out his hand. "Shake on it."

She didn't want to shake on it. His gaze challenged her, and she took his hand. But he didn't play fair. He held her hand, his thumb brushing hers a few times.

"Thank you for making me smile," he whispered, and then he kissed her cheek.

The boys covered their mouths. Willow laughed and walked away, but her insides were shaking because he kept switching things around on her, making her want him in her life.

She opened the cabinet on the carport and pulled out a bag of charcoal and starter fluid. As she walked back, Clint called her a cheater.

"I'm not cheating. Did I not say that I could build a fire?" She piled charcoal under a few twigs of wood and one larger piece. After dousing them with starter fluid she waited a few seconds and struck a match. The charcoal blazed, and the wood sparked, crackled and caught fire.

"Tah-dah."

"You win." Clint stood next to her. "I still say you cheated, but you win."

Willow handed him her stick. "I like mine well-done. And my marshmallows light brown, so that they're just hot enough to melt the chocolate."

"Yes, ma'am." Clint hugged her waist, one arm around her, and his shoulder brushing hers. When he let her go she backed into her chair to watch.

The boys sat one on each side of him and he helped them skewer the hot dogs. Willow's heart ached for the three of them. Their faint conversation drifted back to her and she strained to hear, wiping away tears that trickled down her cheeks.

"Can't we have marshmallows first?" David asked.

"Nope, buddy, we have to eat something good for us."

"Hot dogs aren't good for us," Timmy informed him with a slight shake of his head. "They're full of servatives."

"*Pre*servatives," Clint corrected.

"Yes, those." Timmy lifted his nearly black hot dog out of the fire.

"Here, Timmy, let me help you get that on a bun." Willow walked to the table that held their condiments, chips and bottled water. "Do you want ketchup?"

Timmy shook his head. He looked up at her, eyes watery. "I want my mom, 'cause she knows that I don't like buns, and I just like mustard."

Willow actually felt her heart break. It cracked into a million pieces and flooded her eyes with tears she couldn't blink back fast enough. Timmy was staring at her with a thousand questions in his little eyes, and what could she do?

"Tim, buddy, that isn't fair." Clint's face was a mask of control that Willow knew he couldn't be feeling.

"It's okay." Willow smiled and brushed Timmy's hair back, patting him on the back rather than giving him the hug that she wanted to give, but knew that he didn't want at that moment. She could see it in his stiff little shoulders and the challenge in his eyes.

"Come on, guys, let's eat fast so we can have

s'mores. I love s'mores." Willow squirted mustard on a plate and let Timmy push his hotdog next to it. He reached for a small bag of chips and walked off, still hurting.

David inched closer to her side. He tugged on her hand and she looked down, smiling because he was smiling. "I like my hot dog on a bun."

"Do you like mustard or ketchup?"

He pointed to the ketchup. Willow fixed his plate, and he picked the seat next to hers.

Clint was still facing the fire. Willow wanted to tell him it would be okay. She couldn't. How could she make that promise? Especially when his back was to her, and his shoulders were as stiff as Timmy's, a sign that he was trying too hard to be strong.

The fire flickered, orange and blue flames dancing in the light breeze and shooting sparks into the air that fluttered and died out. It kept Clint in a trance for a few minutes, thinking, praying. The boys were behind him, talking to Willow in soft tones about the sound of the crickets that she couldn't hear, and why they loved s'mores the best, but hot dogs were okay, too.

Kid talk, like everything was okay. And they had no idea that their world hinged on a group of guys thousands of miles away searching for their mother. He sighed and closed his eyes, feeling the heat from the fire blending with the warm summer night and a light breeze.

"Do you want one, Uncle Clint?" Timmy tugged

at his hand, looking up at him with eyes that still questioned.

"Yes, I do want a s'more." He wrapped an arm around his nephew's shoulder and thought back to his own childhood, before his mother died.

A lump of emotion rose from his heart to his throat, and he swallowed it down because he had to make this work for the boys, for their sake. Timmy leaned in close, his hand tighter on Clint's.

"Can we call my mom?" The little boy asked.

"Let's sit down and pray for her instead." Clint sat down in the lawn chair and pulled Timmy onto his lap. "We can't call her right now, but we can say a prayer for her."

"Do you think she will know that we're praying?" Timmy whispered.

"I think she will. And she definitely knows we love her." Clint's silent prayer was that his sister would find faith. Now more than ever.

Timmy nodded against his shoulder, leaning in close and wrapping sticky-marshmallow arms around his neck. Clint couldn't look at Willow. He knew that in the dark there would be tears in her eyes.

He wanted to hold them all. He wanted to hold Jenna, too. A hand touched his arm. Willow. She smiled at him and nodded. He was doing okay.

He prayed, and David climbed onto his lap with Timmy. Willow pulled her chair closer. As the fire burned down to coals, they sat together, singing "Jesus Loves Me."

Clint prayed his own prayers, silent prayers for wisdom. He hadn't hurt this bad since his mother's death. He remembered that day, and the following year, dealing with the pain and no one to really lean on. He hadn't known how to tell anyone how bad it hurt. Willow was sitting next to him, her hand on his arm, and he didn't know how to let her in.

## Chapter Fourteen

Sunday evening the church parking lot was full of people. Willow stopped her truck, parking at the edge of the road, the only space left. The tiny community church, far from town and any real housing development, didn't have need of a big parking area, not on a normal Sunday.

Today wasn't just any Sunday. Today was the day after they had learned that Jenna Cameron was MIA. Today was a day of prayer that she would come home to her sons and her family.

Clint had come early with Janie and the boys. The boys would be in the nursery, far from the service and prayer. Clint had taken Willow's and Janie's advice. The boys didn't need to know.

How would the boys survive this, if Jenna didn't come home? And Clint? Last night sitting next to that fire with the boys, she had watched him struggle. Even after the boys had gone to bed he had insisted that everything was okay. He was fine.

He wasn't fine. He was hanging on to pride, using it as a lifeline. She recognized it because she knew that it had been her stumbling block from time to time.

Janie stood on the steps of the church, waiting for her. Willow smiled at her aunt, who had put off her trip to Florida. Indefinitely. She couldn't go anywhere with Jenna missing.

And then there was Mr. Cameron in the nursing home. He thought Jenna had run away again, like she did every time she didn't like the rules. Willow wiped at her eyes and smiled for her aunt.

"I'm glad you're here. Clint needs you." Janie slipped an arm through Willow's as they walked up the steps.

Willow wanted to disagree about Clint needing her. Clint was so used to being needed, he had a difficult time letting others be strong for him. He was still trying to protect and rescue. This morning she had caught him returning phone calls for her.

For now it didn't matter. He needed the distraction. He couldn't go to Iraq and find his sister. He couldn't make things right. So he was walking around in a stupor, rescuing everyone in sight.

She saw him at the front of the church, no longer himself. He wore khaki pants and a white button-down shirt. She compared him to that cowboy she had met back in May, with the toothpaste smile and eyes that crinkled at the corners.

Today he had the weight of the world on his shoulders. It was a burden he needed to give to God. She knew it was easier said than done.

"She's coming home, Clint." Willow squeezed his hand and let it go.

He touched his lips with his fingers and lowered his hand. THANK YOU. His gray eyes watered, and he looked away.

The pastor walked through a door at the side of the sanctuary, a kind man in his sixties who loved his congregation and treated them all like family. His family. And the compassion in his eyes said that he hurt when they hurt.

Pastor Gray smiled out at the gathering. Willow turned, seeing people she'd never seen before. The pews were crowded. People were lining the walls.

As the pastor spoke, Clint signed the words for Willow. And she let him, because she had to accept what was happening to her hearing. She was learning to let go of pride.

"When we pray, we're to pray believing that God in heaven hears our prayers, and answers our prayers. Sometimes we say we're 'just going to pray about it.' And we make 'just' sound like a last resort. But the word *just* means something very different. It means 'immediately.' It means 'now.'

"'I'm just going to pray' is sometimes our way of saying, 'well, nothing else has worked, I'm just going to pray.' But add the word *immediately* in place of *just*. 'I'm immediately going to pray.' That's what we should do in every situation. Every time we stumble, doubt, or fear, we should 'just pray.'" He paused and smiled. Clint continued to sign, catching up. "And that's what we're going to do now for Jenna Cameron. We're just going to pray."

He stepped out from behind the pulpit. "And we're going to pray, believing our God in heaven hears and answers. We're not going to pray thinking that God might or might not answer. We're going to be the woman who touched the hem of Jesus's garment, knowing in faith that to touch Him would bring healing."

"Amen." Clint whispered the word.

Amen.

Clint stood and Willow walked with him to the altar, aware that others were pushing in around them to pray. It was warm and close. Willow knelt next to Clint, aware that someone had knelt next to her.

I'M TRYING TO HAVE FAITH, Clint signed.

Willow swallowed, nodding, because she understood "trying to have faith." She understood moving forward one day at a time, waiting for that moment when a person realized the meaning, the purpose of a situation and knew they could make it.

WE HAVE TO ASK FOR MORE FAITH. She moved her fingers, silently, words for Clint alone.

MORE FAITH. Clint bowed his head and nodded.

Walking out of the church with the boys, Clint saw Willow standing off to the side waiting for him, her expression soft as her gaze settled on them.

"Do you want to eat dinner with us?" Willow asked as they walked across the lawn to the parking lot. He noticed her truck at the edge of the road. Janie had ridden with him.

Janie rounded up the boys, smiling and talking like everything was normal and that tomorrow would be a fun day. She told them they would even get out the garden hose again. If it didn't rain.

Willow had asked him about dinner. "No, not tonight."

"Clint, you should come to the house. There's no reason to be alone."

"I'm not alone." He looked away.

"There are ways of being alone without being alone." She smiled, but the gesture was weak. "I know from experience. And I know all about using pride to close out the world. I know…"

"I know you do." He wanted to hold her, because she knew how it felt to lose things important to her. Someone important to her. He couldn't imagine her pain in that hospital, alone. He couldn't imagine complete silence.

He felt pretty weak compared to her.

"Don't shut us out, then." That determined lift of her chin.

"I won't shut you out. But I'm going to get the boys to bed early. I'll see you in the morning."

"Okay."

"Willow, I'm fine."

"Of course you are. We women are the only ones who need someone to lean on, right?"

"Something like that," he teased, hoping she'd smile and let it go.

"I'm here if you need me." She let it go, that easily.

"I know you're here."

He watched her walk away, and he was sorry that he'd spent a lifetime hiding his own pain and handling things alone. Janie had always just known, without him telling her.

From the looks of things, her niece didn't think he was a closed book, either. He'd sure never thought of himself as transparent.

On Thursday afternoon the military chaplain called with news. Clint listened to the man on the other end, faceless and practically nameless, telling him that they had leads. They were hopefully optimistic that they would recover Jenna Cameron.

*Hopefully optimistic* and *recover.* Clint tried to push the terms aside, to not think too deeply about what they meant. He was pretty sure the military had meant to give him hope. He reached down deep for faith, because it felt buried by the emotion of the last few days.

Sunday and the prayer meeting felt like a lifetime ago.

The boys were in the barn with Willow. Clint walked through the double doors and headed in the direction of the office. He could hear the boys laughing and Willow talking to them.

He stopped short of entering the office. He couldn't go in there like this, because he knew the boys would see it in his eyes. If they didn't, Willow would.

Deep breath, and he ran a hand through his hair. The

smile he plastered on was for the boys, to keep them smiling. They looked up when he stepped into the room.

They were on the floor, coloring pictures of Black Beauty. Willow was sitting at her desk, a catalogue in front of her.

"What's going on in here?" He sat down opposite Willow.

"The boys are coloring." She smiled at Timmy and David. "I'm picking an Arabian mare from this catalogue."

"You know the guys at the feed store are going to tease you."

She smiled. "They tease me about everything. The feed I buy, the vitamins I give my animals, and I think they make fun of my truck."

He laughed because they did make fun of her truck. "You drive a purple diesel around the country. And then there's your Ford. You have fuzzy dice hanging from the mirror."

"A little girl gave me those dice."

"Tell that to the guys, not me."

"Nope, let them talk." She opened the catalogue and pushed it across the desk. "I like this mare." Eye contact. "Have you heard anything?"

"Yes."

She looked down at her hands, the mood slipping from easy laughter to serious. She glanced at the boys, and he followed the look.

THEY HAVE LEADS AND ARE "HOPEFULLY OPTIMISTIC." Clint signed, I DON'T KNOW WHAT THAT MEANS. BUT

LAST NIGHT DAVID ASKED WHEN HIS MOM WILL CALL. Willow's eyes filled with tears. WHAT DO I SAY TO A QUESTION LIKE THAT?

She shook her head and her hands moved in silent communication. I DON'T KNOW. I'M SORRY.

THEY NEED NORMAL. THEY NEED CHURCH AND THE PARK. I NEED TO TAKE THEM TO THE ZOO OR THE LAKE.

THEN DO IT. KEEP THEM BUSY. She smiled. KEEP YOURSELF BUSY. TAKE THEM BACK TO CHURCH.

Clint glanced back at the boys. They were still coloring, ignoring the silent communication between adults. They had accepted that sometimes signs were used for words.

I'M AFRAID THAT THEY'LL HEAR SOMETHING AT CHURCH.

I KNOW. BUT, CLINT, YOU CAN'T HIDE THEM AWAY HERE. HIDING IS JUST THAT, HIDING. IT'S FEAR AND LACK OF TRUST.

She was right, he signed. He didn't tell her the rest. If he couldn't handle this situation, how would he handle the next fifteen or so years, trying to raise them alone, trying to make the right choices?

WE'RE HAVING FAITH THAT SHE'S COMING HOME. Willow signed with determination. Determined, the way she approached everything in life.

She was facing profound deafness, and yet she didn't seem to waver in her convictions, in her determination and her faith.

"You're right." He stood up, but another catalogue caught his attention. "What's that?"

"Independence." She smiled, her eyes bright, maybe with tears. "I'm facing my future and letting go of pride. There are ways I can help myself to be independent. New phones. Answering machines that change a voice message to a typed message, and a few other gizmos."

"I think that's great. And don't forget, you have friends."

"I won't forget." She smiled up at him, winking in a way that made him want to forget everything. "And don't you forget either."

"Hey guys, let's go riding." He turned back to Willow. "Want to go?"

She did. Smiling, she stood and held a hand out to David. Clint didn't know what he would do without her.

And that thought brought a lot of other questions he wasn't ready to deal with. Questions like—where did she fit into the rest of his life? Did she even want to be there, or were they just friends?

He pushed those questions aside and walked to the tack room to pull out bridles and saddles.

After a long ride, Willow slid to the ground and pulled a groggy David down. He wrapped his arms around her neck and she held him for a minute. When he didn't move, she glanced down and he smiled up, his eyes heavy.

"You need a nap." She pulled him close and held him for another minute before setting him down.

Timmy seemed a little more alert, but not much. Willow smiled at Clint, and he winked. Her heart couldn't take much more of his charm. Cowboys either didn't know their power over women, or else used it so effectively that it came off as innocent and unknowing.

She'd met hundreds over the last five years. And she'd always managed to keep her distance and not be touched by that charm.

Until now.

"I'm going to take these boys home for a nap." Clint was unsaddling the horse he'd ridden and Timmy and David were sitting on the ground, leaning against a stall door.

Willow cross-tied the mare in the center aisle for a good brushing. "Do you want me to brush your horse?"

"No, I can take care of him. What about dinner tonight?"

"What about it?"

He glanced over the bare back of the big old buckskin he'd bought. The horse was faded gold with a black mane and tail. Showy, but solid. A cowboy's horse.

"Dinner. What are you doing? Janie is gone, isn't she?"

"She's with her friends." Willow tossed the currycomb in a bucket and led her horse into the stall. Clint walked up behind her with a scoop of grain. He leaned in past her and filled the bucket.

"Do you want to run into Grove with us?"

"For dinner?" She shrugged.

"You have to eat."

"Yes, I have to. Okay, sure."

"If you don't want to…"

She glanced at the boys, now leaning against each other, eyes closing. "Take them home. And yes, I'll go with you. They have great fried chicken at the new diner."

"Fried chicken it is."

He led his horse away, out the back door to the gate. Willow watched. She glanced back at the boys and Timmy was awake. He gave her a look and then shifted away. When Clint returned, the boys jumped up, grabbing his hands and mumbling goodbye to her.

Willow watched from the barn as Clint headed down the road to the foreman's house, a boy on either side, both leaning against him.

It was a picture she'd like to have hanging on the wall of her office, the cowboy in his faded jeans, T-shirt and white cowboy hat, and two little miniatures walking next to him down a dusty country road. For a minute it almost felt like they belonged in her life in a forever kind of way.

She allowed herself to have that dream, of being loved forever. She thought it might feel like this, like a summer afternoon in the country and a man who was always there. It had been a long, long time since she'd daydreamed of cowboys and forever. Sixteen years to be exact.

It could only be a dream.

She walked across the road to the house, Bell following at her heels, a stick in the dog's mouth. Bell was an optimist, always believing someone would take the hint and throw the stick. Willow leaned and grabbed it from the slobbering dog, regretting it immediately. She tossed the stick and wiped her hands on her jeans. The dog ran across the yard. Rather than bringing the stick back, she took it to a hole she'd dug and lay down with it.

Willow walked up the front steps of the house, listening to quiet country sounds that were even now fading. She sighed, because she didn't want to think about it all being gone.

Silence. She'd spent two days in a world of complete silence until she got new hearing aids. And soon it would be permanent.

She would survive. Because God was with her, always. Even in the silence.

And if there was a miracle, she prayed it was for Jenna, bringing her home to her boys.

Janie wasn't at home. Willow walked through the empty house, thinking about the time when Janie would move. She hadn't allowed herself to really contemplate that day, and what it would mean to her.

Now she did. As she sat in the living room under the gentle push of air from the ceiling fan, she thought about living in this house, in silence. Alone.

She closed her eyes and thought about the business she'd built, and holding on to independence. And for a minute, just a minute, confidence faded and she felt afraid.

She wouldn't be able to hear the telephone or the radio. She wouldn't be able to hear the announcer at bull-riding events.

Everything she'd lost, and would lose, coiled around her heart. Brad. The baby. Now her hearing, and maybe her business. She'd thought Brad would love her forever. She had believed they would have children and a family that laughed together. She had never dreamed she would lose her hearing completely.

Her mind snaked back to thirty minutes ago, thinking about Clint in her life forever. She had let go of those dreams until he walked into her life again. And now, how did she go back to being content with this life she had chosen, living on this ranch, raising bulls and being single?

"God, get me through this," she whispered and closed her eyes. "Give me peace that surpasses all understanding, and show me your will for my life, so that I don't feel so alone."

The fan continued to swish cool air from the air conditioner, and Willow drifted off.

Clint dozed off in the recliner, feet up, two boys on his lap. When he woke up one arm was asleep. The other was empty. He blinked and sat up, sort of. He moved his head and then his arm, the arm Timmy had slept on. Stiff.

He moved it a few times, bending and clenching his fist. David slept on the other arm. He moved the little boy, who moaned and curled up as Clint got out of the chair. He reached for a blanket on the couch and draped it over David.

Timmy. He peeked in the kitchen. No sign of the missing twin. On the way down the hall, toward the bedrooms, he turned the temperature up on the thermostat.

No sign of Timmy in the bedroom. No need to panic. He could picture his nephew sneaking outside to play with Bell, or with toy cars. He couldn't see him wandering too far from the house.

He walked out the front door and stood on the porch. No sign of the missing twin. The yard was dusty from lack of rain, and humidity hung in the air like a wet rug, weighing down the atmosphere. Clint wiped a hand across his already-perspiring brow.

"Timmy!" He cupped his mouth with his hands and shouted into late afternoon silence. "Timmy!"

No answer.

He walked back into the house, the screen door banging behind him. David was sitting in the recliner, holding on to the blanket like it was a lifeline.

"David, do you know where Timmy went?"

David shook his head, but his eyes were big, and Clint wondered.

"David, buddy, this is dangerous. If you know, you have to tell me."

The little boy shook his head again, and tears rolled down his cheeks. Clint didn't blame him. He felt a lot like crying, too. But someone had to be the grown-up. And that seemed to fall on him.

"Come on, let's go to Willow's." Clint picked up David's shoes, and the little boy slid them on. And then he raised his arms to be carried.

Clint walked down the road to Willow's, searching the fields on either side for the figure of a little boy. David clung to his neck, wiry legs wrapped around his waist. The boy sucked his thumb, and Clint didn't stop him.

Timmy could be anywhere. He could be in the barn, or with Willow. He could have gone in with the bulls. Clint told himself Timmy wouldn't do that.

But then again, an hour ago, he wouldn't have thought Timmy would take off while everyone else was sleeping. So where did that put Clint on the parenting scale? Not too high, he figured.

He pounded on Willow's front door, and she didn't answer. That gave him hope. Maybe Timmy had gone to her and the two were together. He knocked again. Still no answer. He pushed the door open and looked in.

Willow was asleep in the living room, stretched out in a chair with her feet on the ottoman. He stepped into the room and hesitated above her, looking down at a face peaceful in sleep and every bit as beautiful as when she was awake.

He knelt, setting David on the edge of the ottoman and reached for Willow's hand. She shifted and then jumped a little. Her smile was sleepy, unguarded.

"Waking me like that could get you hurt." She sat up, pulling her knees to her so that David had more room.

"I can't find Timmy. I woke up from a nap and he was gone."

Willow moved, reaching for the shoes next to her chair. "We'll find him."

"I'm going to head down the road on foot. Could you check the barn?"

She slid on her shoes. "Of course I can. I'll take my cell phone so you can call if you find him."

Willow walked out the barn, David tagging along behind her. She surveyed the fields, and the pens that held bulls. She prayed she wouldn't see him anywhere near the bulls. He knew better. Of course he did.

"David, did your brother say anything about leaving or doing something?"

"No." The child reached for her hand. "He just wants Mom to come home. So do I."

"I know, honey. But did he say something about playing outside, or doing something without telling any of us?"

David shook his head. "No, he just wonders how far away Iraq is."

"It's a long way."

Bell ran out of the barn. Willow reached down to pat the dog. If anyone knew where Timmy was, it was probably Bell. And that didn't do them a lot of good.

She flipped on lights as they walked through the doors of the barn. Something moved, catching her attention. She squinted as her eyes adjusted from bright sunlight to the dim recesses of the barn.

It might have been her imagination, or not. She thought a door closed on one of the stalls, just barely. David's hand was still in hers, and they hurried toward the stall that held her mare.

The horse whinnied, and she heard a thump. Willow let go of David's hand and ran to the stall. She peeked in, afraid of what she might see, afraid that the horse had hurt the child.

The noise had been caused by an overturned bucket. Willow smiled down at Timmy, who was trying to steady the upside-down bucket. The mare had a bridle on her head, the bit under her mouth, not in. No saddle.

"Timmy, what are you doing?"

Timmy frowned at her. "I'm going to find my mom. Uncle Clint is just going to leave her over there lost, and she isn't going to come home if someone doesn't go get her."

Big, brave words and a child's broken heart. How had he found out? Willow opened the door and spoke quietly, reassuring the horse who was trembling and holding steady as the little boy leaned against the mare's side, obviously thinking he could ride her bareback.

Willow picked him up and scooted the bucket out the door. She pulled the bridle off the horse, slid a hand over the mare's neck and then backed out of the stall with the sobbing four-year-old in her arms.

"Shhh, sweetie, it's okay."

Timmy shook his head against her neck, and tears soaked her skin. "I want my mom."

"I know you do." And it was Clint's place to tell the boys everything. Willow reached into her pocket for her phone and speed-dialed Clint's number. When he answered she choked back a sympathetic sob. "He's here, in the barn. He isn't hurt, but he's hurting."

Because somehow he had overheard that his mother was missing.

Clint ran from the main road back to the barn. When he walked through the doors, he took a deep breath and slowed down. He walked toward Willow and the boys.

Timmy and David sat on the bench next to Willow. The boys didn't look at him. Willow shrugged, and her smile wavered. He grabbed the five-gallon bucket next to the bench, turned it over and sat down facing the boys.

"What's up, guys?"

Timmy looked up, his eyes and nose red from crying. He swiped a hand across his face. "I want you to go find my mom."

Clint swallowed and nodded, taking a few minutes to process the comment. "Well, kiddo, I can't do that. I can't go to Iraq. And your mom wouldn't want me to leave you alone."

Clint would have liked nothing better than to hop on a plane and go to Iraq to look for his sister. He couldn't tell that to the boys, or tell them how worried he was.

"We're fine here with Willow." A four-almost-five-year-old's logic. It sounded like it made perfect sense.

"I can't leave you here, partner. And there are real soldiers looking for your mom." How had the boys found out? "Timmy, you have to tell me what's going on. How do you know your mom is lost?"

"Missing. She's missing. I heard the word at church and then when you were talking on the phone. You said she's still missing. And I think guys shouldn't leave sisters alone."

"And I agree. But when guys make a promise, like the one I made to your mom, we have to keep those promises."

David didn't comment.

"David, buddy, do you understand that?"

David shook his head.

"Timmy, do you understand?"

Timmy shook his head. "No. I just want my mom."

"I know, buddy, I know. And I want her to come home. I think we should pray. That's the most important thing we can do, pray."

He held his arms out, and Timmy climbed onto his lap.

They prayed. And Timmy and David added their own prayers to the end, asking God to bring their mom home safe.

As Clint listened, he felt his own faith grow. Kids did that. They made everything seem possible. They had faith…until adults came along and cast seeds of doubt.

It was easy to think of all the negatives, the bad things that could happen, the worst possible outcome.

Clint closed his eyes, refusing to undo the faith with which the boys prayed. And he couldn't look at Willow, because he had prayers of his own that seemed selfish at the moment.

## Chapter Fifteen

Clint walked through the wide double doors at the end of the barn. The shadowy interior was familiar and comforting. Ten days, and Jenna hadn't been found. There had been calls to tell him they were searching, but nothing to give them hope. Nothing to give the boys hope. It wasn't easy for two little boys to go to bed each night, knowing their mom was missing.

A movement at the far end of the barn. Willow pushing a wheelbarrow of grain. She was up early. And she was angry with him. That had been pretty obvious the day before, when he'd heard her struggling with a call and he'd taken over.

He shouldn't have.

He should give her space, because she knew how to take care of herself.

She turned and saw him. She set the wheelbarrow down and stood, waiting. A cowgirl in shorts and a T-shirt. He walked toward her.

"Good morning."

She nodded. "I have coffee in the office."

"I had some." He looked in the stall next to him, at the Arab filly she'd bought. An Arabian. He shook his head, still wondering why she'd done that.

"Stop looking at her like that." Willow walked up next to him. She still smelled like soap and herbal shampoo. Her hair was a little damp.

"Sorry, I'm just not sure what you're going to do with her."

"I think she's pretty." She smiled at him. "It's about endurance, Clint. She can go for hours, and she has a pretty face."

"It's all about a pretty face?"

"She's sweet." She rested her hand on the horse's red-gold neck, and the animal moved closer, nuzzling her shoulder. "See what I mean?"

"Yes, she's sweet."

Not a cow horse.

"You're too set in your ways." She said it and walked off, and he thought she probably meant it in more ways than one.

He opened his mouth to say something, but a shrill ring interrupted.

"Telephone." He nodded toward the office. "The phone is ringing."

She hurried in that direction and he followed. She had picked it up and was talking when he walked into the room. Instead of finishing the conversation, she handed it to him.

"It's someone from the military," she whispered with her hand over the receiver.

He took it, but he didn't lift the phone to his ear. He didn't want to hear. Not this way. Shouldn't they come to his house and tell him in person. Shouldn't there be something more to it than this?

Willow sat on the edge of her desk. She touched his arm. "Answer it, Clint."

He did. "Clint Cameron here."

"Clint, it's me."

He cried. And all his life he'd been taught that only sissies cried. He could hear his dad telling him to stop that bawling. But real men cried when they heard the voice of their sister for the first time in weeks. Real men cried when prayers were answered.

"Clint?" Her voice sounded weak.

"Jenna. Where are you?"

"I'm on my way to a hospital in Germany."

"Where? I'm coming over there."

She laughed, a soft, fluttery and weak sound. "No, you're not. You're not dragging the boys over here. Not here, Clint. Give me time."

"What happened?"

"It's a long story, but I was safe."

"Where have you been?"

"Safe. I'll tell you more when I see you."

"You're okay?" He sat down on the desk next to Willow. He was shaking, and Willow's hand was on his arm. The long pause, static on the line, and the sound of chopper blades, all felt like chaos in his stomach.

"I'm going to be okay. It's going to take time." She sobbed, and he couldn't stand it. "They're not sure about my leg, Clint."

He didn't cry this time. He had to be strong. He had to be able to take care of her. "I'm coming over there."

"No, you're not. You're going to take care of the boys until I can come home. When I get to the States you can come and see me."

"I don't know."

"You have to agree." She paused, a long pause. "If you come over here, I'll give up and let you take care of me."

"I love you, Jen."

"I love you, too. I've been praying for you."

She was praying for him. She was lost, far from home, and she'd prayed for him. How long had he prayed for her to find faith?

"We prayed for you, too."

"You didn't tell the boys, did you?"

He looked at Willow, remembering that she wouldn't let him. "No, I didn't tell the boys."

The boys found out on their own. He would tell her later, not now when she needed to think of herself and getting better.

"Good. I'll call again later, and I want to talk to them."

"They've missed you. We've all missed you."

"Are you in love yet?" He could hear her smile when she asked the question.

"You've got to let it go."

"So, you are." She breathed deep and he heard engines rumbling and people talking. "I'm praying you'll let someone love you."

He glanced away from Willow. "I love you, Jenna."

"Chicken."

She said goodbye, and he set the phone down on the desk. She was safe. She was going to need him more than ever.

"This is definitely a good day." Willow hopped down from the desk, her smile radiant.

"She said her leg is bad. What does that mean?"

The smile she'd worn faded, and she shrugged, her eyes shadowing for a minute.

"Whatever it means, I know she'll get through it with your help. She's alive, and she's coming home to her boys." She hesitated. "And from my end of that conversation, it sounds like she's strong."

"She is." He remained on the edge of the desk. "She's stronger than I am."

"You're human. She knew she was alive. You didn't."

He nodded, because he hadn't thought about it that way. "I'm going to work those two-year-old bulls."

"Not today, Clint. Take time with the boys. Let them know that their mom is coming home to them."

"You'll need help."

"No, actually, I can take care of things around here." Her smile this time was a little tense. "Remember, I've been doing that for a while."

"There are a few messages on the answering

machine, calls that need to be returned." He knew that Janie used to make those calls, but Willow had been pushing Janie back, reminding her that she had to do this on her own.

"Clint, I can do this."

"I know you can."

She frowned and pointed to the door, pointing him to the exit. "Try saying it like you mean it."

"I don't want to fight with you."

"I'm not fighting. I'm taking care of my business. I'm holding on to my life and my future. And I'm going to tell you now, when Jenna comes home, you're going to have to let her do things for herself."

"I know that, Willow."

She shook her head, and by then he was angry with her. But from the snarly look on her face, she was pretty mad herself.

"No, you don't. You take over. Whether you mean to or not, you do. From the moment you learned about my hearing, you changed. You started treating me like I'm a different person. And I'm not."

"I'm going to spend that time with the boys. I'll talk to you later."

"Clint?"

He lifted a hand as he walked out of the room. He didn't have time to work this out with her, not when he had the boys—and Jenna coming home wounded. If he'd been taking over, now was the time to back out and let her have the reins back.

He could do that, no problem.

* * *

Clint was avoiding her, had been avoiding her since the phone call from Jenna. Three days, and they'd barely talked. She could think of reasons why. He was mad at her, maybe for telling him to give his sister room. Or maybe he'd realized, after returning calls for Willow, and having to repeat things when he spoke to her, that even a friendship with her required too much work.

He wouldn't be the first person to make that decision. And now she had additional baggage that came with a relationship. Her worsening condition. And no children. She touched her stomach because today was the anniversary of the accident.

It didn't hurt the way it had once hurt, thinking of her baby, and knowing that she would never again experience that thrill of life growing inside her belly.

God was helping her to move forward, and giving her new joys. The twins counted as a joy. They were a blessing she didn't want to miss out on.

Willow poured food in the cat's bowl and walked out of the barn. She stood outside the building, enjoying a cool breeze and the sweet smell of rain in the air.

They needed rain, desperately. Her gaze traveled to the foreman's house. Clint was running around the yard, shooting the boys with a water gun. She smiled at the sight of them together, happy again.

Yesterday he'd brought them over for some of Janie's homemade ice cream. It had been a celebration, with sparklers for the Fourth of July, and because Jenna would be coming home.

Prayers answered. Willow walked across the road and stopped near the swing. Not forsaken.

She looked up, amazed by the dark clouds eating up the blue. They hadn't had rain for three weeks. They needed moisture, not a gully washer that would hit the ground and run off before it could soak in.

Rather than going inside, she sat down on the swing to watch the storm approach. The breeze stirred the leaves in the tree. A piece of paper someone had dropped bounced across the lawn. The temperature dropped a good ten degrees.

Willow looked up, watching the stirring in the clouds with interest. With the temperature dropping this fast, it could get bad. And she had animals in the field. She got up and hurried back to the barn, remembering a cow that hadn't come up for feeding time. Knowing this cow, Willow knew without a doubt that she'd gone off somewhere alone to have her calf. Of course the cow would do that with a storm coming.

She hurried through the barn, eager to get to the other end, and a clear view of the southern sky. If tornadoes were forming, they would form in the southwest and move northeast. The pattern was nearly a given.

When tornado season hit, she always tried to remind herself that the storms seemed to hit the same areas over and over again. It was a phenomenon she didn't understand. But she also knew that nothing in life was for certain.

Her Arab filly poked a nose over the stall door

and whinnied as Willow passed. "Hey, sweetheart, it'll be okay."

The wind whipped, blowing a door, banging it so hard that Willow heard and jumped. The horse skittered to the back of the stall. Willow turned in the direction of the noise. Nothing but the wind.

Her old farm truck was parked out back. She pushed a hat on to her head, grabbed a horse blanket, and rope and ran for the truck. Rain was starting to fall and she didn't want to think of the cow out there alone, laboring with a calf that might be too big to be delivered.

Huge drops of rain pelted the windshield as she drove through the gate and down into the field. She had to get out and close the gate behind her. When she got back into the truck, she was soaked. She shifted from neutral to first gear and let the truck coast through the field as she searched for the cow.

A few minutes later she spotted the animal in a small stand of trees, obviously laboring to have a calf that wasn't going to be easy to deliver. Willow parked and jumped out of the truck. The heifer gave her a pitiful look that begged for help.

"Oh honey, we're in big trouble." The feet of the calf were showing. The cow looked exhausted with her sides heaving, like she'd been at this for awhile.

And the rain began to fall in earnest.

Willow wrapped the rope around the hooves of the calf as the cow went to her knees, exhausted from labor. "Poor baby, you're just not going to be able to get this one out yourself."

It wasn't the first calf that Willow had needed to pull. It wouldn't be the last. Every year there were several that needed her help, and sometimes the help of a veterinarian.

Now to get the baby out and back to the dry barn.

A movement a short distance away caught her attention. She turned as Clint ran toward her, hunkering down in the rain, his hat tilted.

"What are you doing out here?" he shouted as he moved in closer, his gaze landing on the cow.

"I had to check on her, and I found her like this."

"You could have asked for help."

"Where are the boys?" Willow continued to work, and Clint moved in close, kneeling on the soggy ground next to her.

"They're with Janie. She got home a few minutes ago." He grabbed the rope and made an adjustment on the knot she had tied. "It'll slip loose."

"I've done this before."

"I know you have, but it's pouring down rain, and I'm here. You could get in the truck and wait."

"Get in the truck?" She blinked a few times, and then wiped the rain from her face. "You're telling me to get in my truck? This is my cow, and I know how to do this. She isn't the first cow that I've had down, and not the first one that I've dealt with alone."

"It's pouring, you're soaked and that lightning is getting close."

"I'm not leaving." She pushed in next to him to prove her point.

"Fine, be stubborn." He grabbed the hooves of the calf and slipped his hands down. "Pull when I say to pull."

"I've done this before." She shouted over the wind and the crash of thunder. He shot a look back and shook his head.

Twenty minutes later the calf was on the ground, and the mother, exhausted but alive, turned to nudge her offspring. Birth. Willow always cried after a birth, whether it was a cow, horse or a litter of kittens in the barn. The miracle of birth moved her. It deepened a longing that she tried to ignore.

"We need to get them to the barn." Clint ran to the truck and grabbed another length of rope. The rain had slowed to a steady mist, but they were both soaked, and their feet sloshed through the soppy mud under the stand of trees where the cow had taken shelter. It hadn't proved to really be a shelter, but the cow didn't know better.

"I'll lead her to the barn." Willow took the rope from his hands. "You drive the calf on up in the truck."

Clint stood in front of her, his gaze holding hers. "Why do you keep pushing me away?"

"I'm not. I'm doing what I've been doing for five years. I'm taking care of my animals, and I'm not letting you take over."

"You're pushing me away."

"I'm sorry you feel that way. I feel like I'm standing my ground and holding on to something that is important to me." She bit down on her lip, waiting for him to say something. She was waiting for him to understand how afraid she was. But she couldn't say it out loud.

She couldn't tell him about her fears. She was afraid of the eventual silence. And she was afraid of losing him. What would he think if she told him that? Especially now, with Jenna coming home and needing him.

She just looked at him, wanting him to get it. And wanting him to make walking away easy.

He didn't say anything. Instead he leaned forward, keeping his hands at his side, and he kissed her. His lips were wet from rain and cool air. Willow closed her eyes, realizing that the storm had nothing on this, on whatever connected them. She wanted to explore it, figure it out.

And she wanted to run from it, before it consumed her and then left her empty.

He pulled back, leaving her cold and uncertain, shivering in rain-soaked clothes. "I'm sorry that you are so determined to push me away," he whispered. She didn't hear, but she read his lips.

"I'll meet you back at the barn." She slipped the rope around the cow's neck.

"Willow, I'm trying to say something here. Are you going to walk away?"

"I'm not sure what I'm doing, Clint. I didn't want you to know about my hearing because I didn't want you to change. I didn't want you to start treating me differently." She held tight to the rope and blinked as she focused on his face. "But things have changed."

She waited for him to answer, to tell her that he would let her be herself. She wanted him to do something to show her things hadn't changed.

And as she waited, she saw their friendship melting away because he didn't understand. For him, being strong seemed as natural as breathing. And for her, it was like struggling for every breath.

I CAN'T DO THIS ANYMORE, he signed. I CAN'T.

"Can't what?"

"Never mind, we need to get back to the house." Clint gave her his jacket. "Since you insist on being the one to walk her to the barn."

Willow nodded, but she didn't know what to say.

He said something she didn't catch.

"What?" She faced him, faced the gray eyes that sometimes flashed with humor, or simmered with some indiscernible emotion. This time the look simmered.

"Willow, whether you want to admit it or not, things are going to change. For all of us. So you find faith, and you learn how to deal with it, but you can't keep it from happening." He exhaled and shook his head. "My sister had part of her leg amputated. She's a single mom with twin boys. Everything is changing. And what you're going through isn't fair, either. If I could fix you all…"

"Clint, you don't have to fix us."

"That isn't what I meant."

She nodded, but she didn't know what to say. And her mind went back to his comment about not being able to take this, and it reminded her of someone about to walk away. He thought she needed to be fixed.

And all she really needed was to be loved for who she was.

"Willow?"

"We should go." She glanced over her shoulder, at more black clouds rolling their way. "Looks like we're about to get hit by more rain."

"You're running from me."

She wished it wasn't true, but it probably was. His eyes reflected the storm, and his smile had disappeared. He deserved some kind of explanation.

"I want you for a friend, not a caretaker."

"Sometimes we're stronger when we let someone help us."

"But you're taking over. You see me as someone you need to fix."

She waited for him to tell her he'd give her space and that he could be in her life without taking over. But instead he took a step back, a step away from her. She saw it in his eyes, realization. He knew that she was right. He sighed and turned away.

The rain started to fall again, this time a gentle, soaking rain. Willow pulled her jacket collar up as he walked away.

He got into the truck and she started up the hill, the cow walking behind her and the truck just ahead. She could see Clint's reflection in the rearview mirror as he kept an eye on them. And she knew that everything changed today.

She had pushed someone from her life, someone who had become maybe her best friend, and it hurt. It hurt worse than that moment when Brad told her their marriage was over. It hurt worse than the plane ride when she was ten years old.

This hurt deep in her heart, like an ache that might linger for a long, long time. And all she had wanted was for him to say he could be in her life without taking over.

Maybe he couldn't.

## Chapter Sixteen

"Why aren't you talking to Clint?" Janie asked after two days of silence. Willow had wondered when her aunt would bring it up.

"I'm not *not* talking to him."

"Okay, then what is this? He came back from helping you with that cow, and since then the two of you have been circling like wasps that have had their nests messed with."

Willow sort of chuckled and smiled. "That's a nice visual image."

"Okay, so, tell me what is going on."

"He's a macho cowboy who likes to fix people. I don't need to be fixed, and I told him that."

"Tell him you love him."

Willow picked up her purse. "I'm not going to tell him I love him. Years ago I had a crush. Now I don't know what I have. I do know that I need to run into town."

"You're stubborn."

Willow nodded. "Yep, I am. Need anything from the store?"

Janie shook her head and walked off. Willow walked out to her truck, patting her leg as an invitation for Bell to ride along.

When she pulled into the feed store in town, an older farmer waved and headed in her direction. Bart Jenson. She took in a deep gulp of air and mentally prepared herself for a man who just couldn't handle the idea that she raised bulls. It wasn't proper he had said, more than once.

"Mr. Jenson." She closed the door of her truck and smiled. He didn't smile back.

"I want to talk to you about the fence of yours that borders my property."

"Didn't we already settle this?"

A truck pulled into the parking lot. Clint's truck. Oh, she so didn't need this. She needed to handle Bart and pay for her grain so it could be delivered on Monday. She didn't need to settle an old dispute all over again.

Clint was getting out of his truck. The windows were down, and the boys waved from the back seat.

"I settled it with that stubborn aunt of yours, but now you own the place." Bart's voice was as growly as his personality. He hitched his thumbs in the straps of his bib overalls and put on his benevolent face, the one he used when talking down to a woman.

Clint was heading their way. To take over. She knew that look on his face. He thought she needed to be rescued.

"I'm sticking with the agreement, Bart. I'm paying for one thousand feet of fence. I'll have it finished by the end of August."

Bart turned away from her. "I'll just talk to Clint about it."

Willow wanted to stomp. She wanted to demand that the older farmer talk to her. And he was ignoring her, waiting for Clint. Willow waited, too, ready to be angry and to tell Clint that he didn't need to fix this for her.

"Clint, I want to discuss this fence situation with you."

"It isn't my fence, Bart."

"Yes, but you know as well as I do that this woman don't know a thing about how this should be done."

"Sounds to me like she does."

Clint smiled and then he tipped his hat and walked away. Willow tried to thank him, but he kept going, and she knew that meant more than words. Bart Gordon was red in the face and looked like a man about to blow. Willow faced the problem, her problem, but her gaze shifted back to Clint, walking through the door of the feed store.

"Bart, I'm sticking with the deal. I keep my word, and I'm asking you to keep yours."

"My word is good, young lady. But I'll have you know, this is the last time we'll do a deal like this."

"Have it your way." She smiled. "But we're going to be neighbors, and we're going to have to work through problems from time to time."

"You won't last on that ranch by yourself, not without Clint or Janie to take care of things."

He stormed off, and Willow wanted to remind him that she'd taken care of herself for five years before Clint Cameron showed up. She could still handle things on her own.

But the thought wilted inside her, because she was having a hard time believing. She knew, without a doubt, that she was going to need help running the ranch.

She knew that she would miss Clint. And he had just proved that he could let her handle things alone. She would have told him, but when he walked out to his truck, he passed by without speaking to her.

And tomorrow he was leaving the boys with them so that he could visit Jenna in the hospital. He planned on being gone for close to a week. Willow started her truck and backed out of the parking space without going in for feed.

Clint walked down the hallway of the hospital, the antiseptic smell so strong he could nearly taste it. He glanced down at the number on a piece of paper the lady at the information desk had given him.

He neared room 512 and his heart ka-thumped in his chest. He could count on one hand the times in his life that he'd been afraid. This one counted.

He paused at the door, giving himself a minute to breathe and to be the older brother Jenna needed. Funny that Willow was pushing him away because she thought he was strong, and because he had a habit of taking over. He felt anything but strong. He shoved the paper into his pocket, practiced a smile and walked into the room.

Jenna was awake and looking at the door, like she'd known he was there. She smiled, a little weary, kind of sad. He took a few steps, aware that they were both on the verge of tears.

"Hey, Sis." He leaned, pulling her to him in a hug that was awkward for them both.

"Let me go now, Clint, you're suffocating me."

He let go and backed up. He was suffocating everyone he cared about. Suffocating the people he loved. He took off his hat and sat down in the seat next to hers.

"Are you okay?" Jenna reached for his hand.

"I've had better days. But I'm here for you."

She laughed, shaky and weak from painkillers. "Clint, are you always going to be there for everyone?"

"I'm sure gonna try."

A light squeeze on his hand. "I'm glad you've always been there for me."

He nodded, and his gaze shifted down to her leg, the amputation a success, they had said. He didn't know how losing part of her leg could be a successful surgery. He was just glad she was alive. And she had faith. Both were answers to prayer.

"I'm going to be okay." She made it sound like a fact.

"I know you are."

"I think I probably feel better than you do."

"I don't know." He leaned forward, resting his hat on his knee. "What happened?"

"I don't remember a lot, but I woke up in sort of a house. An older lady, she'd been a nurse a long time ago, had watched the attack on our convoy. When she saw me, alive, she sent her nephew to drag me to her house. She wanted to save me."

"She did, didn't she?"

"I think so." Tears slid down her cheeks. "I don't like to think about what could have happened."

"Then we won't. Instead let's talk about getting you back home, back to the boys and the farm."

"It's going to be a little while before that happens."

"I know." He touched her brow, brushing back dark hair that fell into her eyes. "But we have you. That's what matters."

"How are my boys?" Tears flooded her eyes. "Can you bring them soon?"

"I will. And they're fine. They're with Janie and Willow. They're probably eating too much ice cream and running the house." He pulled folded pages from a coloring book out of his pocket, along with snapshots of the boys. "They sent these for you."

She took the papers and opened them, tears trickling down her cheeks as she stared at her boys, smiling from the photographs that he hadn't thought to take. The pictures had been Willow's idea.

"They're doing great, Jenna. They miss you, but they're good."

"Thank you for taking care of them for me." She wiped at her eyes with a tissue she pulled from a box on the table. "Are they okay, Clint? Do they know what happened?"

"They're doing great. And they've taken care of me most of the time." He sat forward in the chair. "They do know. They have a lot of questions and suggestions."

They both smiled at that.

"I miss them so much."

"They miss you." And he told her about Timmy's near-escape when he went to look for her.

She smiled, a little bigger, a little more genuine. "Now, I want to talk about you and Willow."

Of course his misery was what she needed to cheer herself up. He nearly laughed, yet he didn't feel like laughing. He definitely didn't want to talk about Willow, who was barely speaking to him.

He had a problem with relationships. He'd known it since high school. He'd had a habit of dating girls who needed to be fixed. The worst mistake had been the judge's daughter. She'd been angry with her parents, and he'd been a good way to get back at them.

After it was over he realized he hadn't loved her after all, because he hadn't really missed her. She'd hurt his pride more than anything.

He missed Willow. Even though he saw her daily at the farm, he missed her.

"Come on, Clint, give it a chance." Jenna tugged at his hand.

"Do you really need to go in that direction to be happy?" He smiled and she laughed.

"Yes, I do. Tell me all about it."

"She thinks I have a habit of taking over."

Jenna laughed. "And you think you don't? Clint, you always take over. It's a big part of your macho personality."

"Fine, I take over. But I can't change who I am, and I don't have time for a relationship."

"Did you want a relationship?" Her laughter was gone, and she looked too serious. "When are you going to let yourself have time?"

"Jenna, I can't think about that right now. I need to think about you and the boys."

She struggled to sit up, and when he reached to help, she put a hand out to stop them. "Hold it right there, Cowboy. See, that's your problem. I can get up by myself. I have to learn to do this on my own. And you can't take over."

"I wasn't."

"You were. You've always taken care of me. And I let you. Now you're trying to take care of Willow. You're a pretty hard guy to fight off, and maybe she's afraid she'll lose."

"I was just trying to help."

"Help by letting us be strong. Help me by realizing that I'm a grown woman with two boys that I have to take care of. Willow has built a business without your help."

"Her hearing is getting worse."

"So, help her to be strong. You can do that. And you have to build your own life. A life that doesn't include taking care of me, the boys or Dad."

It took a minute for that to sink in, and when it did, it hurt. He'd always taken care of Jenna. And now, when she needed him more than ever, she was telling him to back off. She was his little sister. He didn't think he could.

"Clint, let me take care of myself, and I promise, when I need help, I'll ask." She handed him a piece of paper. "And I bet if you ask Willow, she'll tell you that she's willing to ask when she needs help."

"It isn't easy." Changes, they were all facing changes. And if he wanted to keep Willow in his life, he had to be willing to change.

"You're right, it isn't easy. You're a great brother, a great person, but your relationships have always been about taking care of someone. That isn't really love." She pointed to the paper she'd handed him. "That's my life, right there on that paper. I wrote up a one-year plan, a five-year plan and a fifteen-year plan. That's where I want to be and what I want to do. I have goals. I have dreams of my own."

He looked at the list. It included being a mom, taking care of herself and her children and raising horses. Taking care of herself. She had underlined that goal.

He nodded, but it sure wasn't easy. "Good plans."

"Yes, they are. And you need to make a few plans of your own." She smiled, his little sister, strong and a force to be reckoned with. "Plans that don't include taking care of me."

"I'm being lectured." He shook his head at this fact.

"Yes, you are. I think that I have to give you a push so that you'll let me take the steps I need to in my own life. And when you go home, make nice with Willow and let her love you back. Give her room to breathe."

He sat back, realizing what she was telling him. He had been acting like everyone else in Willow's life, taking over and making decisions for her. He should have concentrated on the one thing he realized he really wanted to do.

He wanted to love her.

But he didn't know if she'd be willing to let him. She had walls, and because of him, the walls were now a little higher, and harder to climb.

The phone rang. Willow didn't want to mess with it so she let it go to voice mail. She ignored Janie's questioning look.

"Don't you want to take that?"

Willow shook her head and walked over to the table where the boys were coloring horse pictures that she had printed off the computer. Clint had been gone for four days.

She didn't want to think about missing him or why she missed him. The boys missed him. They had cried last night, and she had come close to crying with them.

This was tougher than being thirteen and falling in

love with an image, someone she didn't really know. That had been a crush, built around a fictional cowboy with Clint's face.

This was different. This went deeper, because now she knew the cowboy. She had held his hand. He had held her.

Letting go of the real thing would be harder than letting go of the dream she'd built all those years ago.

But she had other things to think about. She had an event in a week. She had young bulls that needed to be sold.

Her heart was breaking. That was the hardest thing to come to terms with. She hadn't expected it to happen this way, with her missing Clint and feeling as if she had missed out on something.

"Willow, why are you doing this to yourself?" Janie's question was soft. Willow didn't know if her aunt was whispering, or if it was a bad day.

She turned, smiling for her aunt. "I don't know what you mean."

"You're ignoring phone calls. You're ignoring my questions about what happened between you and…"

Willow raised a hand to stop her aunt. The boys were coloring, but she knew they heard and paid attention to everything. They were smart little guys.

"Let's go outside," Janie suggested, motioning to the front door.

Willow followed, telling the boys to keep coloring, and to not forget their juice. She moved the juice boxes closer and ruffled the hair of each boy as she walked out.

Janie was waiting for her. Waiting, and Willow knew that everything she'd thought about over the last week had to be said.

"Janie, it's time for you to let go. You need to move to Florida. You can't let that condo sit there empty."

"I'll go when I'm ready. But right now, you need me, and Jenna is going to need me."

"We'll both be fine, I bet. And if we need you, we'll call. But you have to go, or you'll regret letting this pass you by."

"Do you regret, Willow?"

"I don't know what that means." She sat down on the porch swing and kicked to make it rock. Janie took the seat opposite. "Do I regret what?"

"Do you regret that you pushed Clint away?"

Willow kicked the swing again to keep it moving. Janie reached out and stopped the momentum. "Don't ignore me."

"I'm not. I need time to think. I don't believe I pushed him away. I made a decision. Janie, when he learned about my hearing, he changed. He started treating me like an invalid."

"Then talk to him."

"I did. He can't help himself. He takes over. That's who he is. And I'm me. I can't stop being the person that I am, just to let him be the tough guy."

"What are you going to do with this place if you don't have help? You're going to have to have someone, so why not Clint?"

"Because that isn't how I want him in my life,

taking over, making decisions for me. Taking care of me."

She wanted him to love her. She had gained so much in the last few years. She had gained faith, and friends. She had confidence in herself, and in her abilities. She had a business that she loved.

And Clint. He had to be included in the things she had gained. And lost.

"Janie, it isn't unusual for me to have people in my life who can't handle my deafness. Maybe Clint can't handle it. It does mean a whole different kind of relationship."

"Some people can't handle it, Willow. But when God brings the right person that person will be able to handle it."

Clint. That's the person Janie meant. And Willow wanted it to be so. But she blocked the thought because she didn't want to be hurt again. Another broken heart, and the world would run out of duct tape.

"I've considered selling the bulls," Willow admitted, and it hurt to say it out loud for the first time. It didn't feel right.

"Oh, Willow, you stubborn girl. You'd rather sell the bulls than ask for help."

"I don't know."

Janie moved to the swing and patted Willow's knee. "Will you pray about this? Don't rush into something and then have more regrets."

"I've been praying."

"And you think this is the right choice, the right direction to take?"

"I don't know yet." She had to take each day as it came. "I'm not sure how to feel or what to do."

A delivery van rumbled down the road, interrupting their conversation. Willow stood as the van stopped and the driver got out. He hurried up the walk, and she held on to Bell, who had a distaste for men in brown uniforms.

"Willow Michaels?" he asked, looking at the package to read her name. Her regular driver knew that without asking.

"Yes."

"Package. Sign here." He held up the electronic clipboard, she signed and he handed over a box.

"What is it?" Janie asked as Willow walked back across the porch.

"No idea."

"Open it."

"I am." Willow slid her fingernail down the side of the box, loosening the tape. She pulled out a box and realized it was from the catalogue she'd been looking at days ago.

She opened the box and looked at the phone, the very phone she had circled in her catalogue. Her eyes watered as she read over the typed gift card inside the box. "Because you can do all things through Christ who strengthens you. This is a step forward."

"Clint did this," she whispered.

Janie patted her arm. And Willow didn't know what

to say. It had always felt as if he was taking over. But now he was giving her freedom. He was giving her room to breathe, to be strong.

"He's a good man, Willow."

"I know he is."

"Okay, we'll both make hard choices. I'm going to plan on leaving for Florida at the end of August, after I go to Texas and spend a week or so with Jenna. That's the date I'm giving myself. Now, your turn."

Willow laughed, Janie made it seem so easy. "I don't know which to tackle first, the bulls or Clint."

"Both." Janie smiled. "Follow the old saying, 'take the bull by the horns.'"

"That's dangerous."

"What are you afraid of?"

"Loving him and losing myself. Or loving him and not being able to give him everything."

"That isn't love, Willow. You find yourself when you fall in love. But you won't know if you don't give it a chance."

Willow nodded but she wondered how she could give love a chance when she knew what her future held and what she wouldn't be able to give to a relationship.

No one was at home. Clint opened the door after knocking a few times and peeked inside. Silent. He walked out to the garage. Janie's Cadillac was gone. Willow's truck was there. Janie must have taken the boys somewhere. So where was Willow?

On the way home from Texas he had felt his insides tensing, but in a way he hadn't experienced before. He'd had that keyed-up feeling on bulls, just before the gate opened. But this was different. This feeling felt a lot like going home to someone that he missed. And hadn't expected to miss, not like this.

She was in the corral with her new mare. She stood in the center of the arena, the horse on a lunge line, trotting in a wide circle. He watched the two work, the woman and the horse. Willow whistled, and the mare changed from a trot to slow gallop. She must have sensed him watching her, because she turned and smiled. The smile was reserved, as if she had questions.

He had questions, too.

She spoke to the horse, and the mare stopped, standing still, legs square and ears alert. He had to admit she'd made a good choice with the Arabian. Willow walked up to the horse, spoke softly, petting the mare's neck, and then she turned and walked up to the fence. The horse walked at her side.

"Welcome home." She acted as if she didn't know what to expect from him. "Janie took the boys to Tulsa to shop for school clothes."

"I see."

"How is Jenna?"

"Strong. Like you." He hoped that would thaw the ice. It helped a little. She smiled.

Funny, he had thought he was rescuing her. But she had rescued him. She had introduced him to what it felt like to fall in love. And now he had to wonder if she was going to let him tell her.

"Thank you for the phone." She leaned against the fence. He opened the gate and walked through to join her.

"Is it the one you wanted?"

"It is. You were snooping in my office again."

"I confess, I snooped." Distracted, he rubbed the mare's velvety face. "Willow, I want you to know that I'm not trying to take over."

She laughed and he looked up, meeting blue eyes that melted his heart. "You were."

"Yeah, maybe I was. I'm kind of used to taking care of people."

"Being taken care of isn't the problem. You taking over like you think I can't take care of myself, that's the problem."

"I know, and I'm working on that. I've always been a fixer. But you don't need to be fixed." He ducked under the head of the horse and stood next to Willow. The mare pushed at him, so he took the lead rope and tied her to a post.

"No, I don't. But I'm working on letting people help me." She smiled up at him, and he felt his world coming undone. Maybe, just maybe, he could be the cowboy who took care of her forever.

If he asked, would she say yes?

Willow slipped her hands into his and waited, expectantly, for him to give her a hint that maybe, just maybe this could last. She had prayed for this moment, for God to show her if this man would be the one who wouldn't walk away.

She hadn't realized how much she wanted that, not until the phone arrived and she realized that as much as he had seemed to be taking over, he did know when to back away.

He had listened to her. And he knew to let her be strong.

"I'm sorry, Willow. I didn't give you the credit you deserve. You're smart and beautiful and strong, and you don't need me to rescue you."

"Sometimes I do, Clint." She enjoyed saying it, enjoyed the widening of his gray eyes and the tender smile that chased away his frown, and dissolved the worry lines that had gathered at the corners of his mouth.

"How often?"

"How often do I need you to rescue me?" She smiled. "Maybe more often than I realized. Clint, sometimes I'm really afraid of what is happening. I'm afraid of the silence. And I'm afraid of being alone."

He took off his hat and dropped it over a post. His gray eyes were intense, holding her gaze. He smiled a little.

"That's honest," he said. "Thank you for that."

"I guess it's time for honesty. Right?"

"Right. I'm glad you might need to be rescued, because I have something my mind." He tangled his fingers in the hair at the back of her neck and pulled her close, his touch gentle and her heart teetering on the edge.

"Really? What?"

"I have forever on my mind." He signed the words as he spoke.

"Okay, we can talk about forever," she whispered, her hand on his arm, pulling him even closer, needing him closer. She liked that his scent was as familiar to her as rain on a summer morning. "Why do you have forever on your mind?"

And she was afraid, because there needed to be more honesty between them.

"Because I can't think of forever without you."

All the right words, but she'd heard those words before. "Clint, have you really thought about this, about my hearing, about babies?"

She choked on those words, and he pulled her closer, holding her so that her cheek was against the warmth of his neck and his arms were strong around her waist.

"I've thought about everything, Willow. And I can't think of anything but loving you." He pulled back, but his hands remained on her waist. "Willow, would you consider loving a cowboy who has a bad habit of rescuing the women in his life?"

"Do you rescue a lot of women?"

He leaned, his forehead touching hers. Willow closed her eyes as his hands moved up her arms to rest on her shoulders. His touch was gentle, his hands calloused but familiar.

"I'd like to think about having only one woman to rescue for the rest of my life, and hers."

"Do you have a certain woman in mind?" Her eyes were still closed.

His lips touched hers, gentle, persuasive, letting her know in no uncertain terms what woman he wanted to rescue for the rest of his life.

And she wanted to be rescued.

He kissed her one last time, and then he pulled away. Willow opened her eyes, still dazed, still trying to think about forever with this man.

"I do have a woman in mind." He kissed her again, at the corner of her mouth and then on her temple. "And I want to make a promise that I'll only rescue you when you need to be rescued." He smiled. "And maybe sometimes when you need it, but don't think so. But I promise to listen when you tell me I'm taking over, and I promise to back off and give you space to be strong."

"I like that idea. If you'll agree to let me rescue you every now and then."

He smiled and pulled her close again. "You already rescued me."

"I like the idea of forever." With a cowboy whose heart was true, and who loved her completely. "We can rescue each other."

And it was just like her dream sixteen years earlier. She had a forever-cowboy, one whose heart was true, and who didn't walk away.

* * * * *

*Be sure to look for the next book
in Brenda Minton's Cowboy series,
THE COWBOY NEXT DOOR,
coming in June 2009,
only from Love Inspired.*

Dear Reader,

When I think of Willow Michaels, I think of all the strong women that I know, or have known. I want to be one of those women, someone who trusts God and overcomes. I want to be Peter, willing to step out of the boat and walk on water, even if I do sink from time to time. To be that strong woman, we need to learn to trust God, believing He is, and that He is able. We also need to trust ourselves, the decisions we make and our ability to handle difficult times or situations. Sometimes we let ourselves down, or we even feel as if God has let us down. At times the people we counted on, or trusted, knowingly or unknowingly let us down. That doesn't mean the end of the road. It's merely a starting place, a detour, a new route that we hadn't expected.

We move on. We forgive. We rebuild. In the process, we grow. In A COWBOY'S HEART, Willow is like so many of us: she's walking that walk of faith, stumbling, but getting back up again.

Pray hard, stand strong.

*Brenda Minton*

# QUESTIONS FOR DISCUSSION

1. Willow Michaels lost a child, her husband, and now she's facing complete and profound deafness. Situations that we encounter cement our faith, making it personal. What milestone in your life created that moment when your faith became real and tangible for the first time?

2. Willow is embarrassed when Aunt Janie reintroduces her to Clint Cameron at the rodeo, because she'd had a crush on him when they were younger. Have you ever been faced with a person from your past? How did you handle it? Was it easy? Awkward?

3. Willow tries to avoid discussing her hearing loss. But avoiding a situation won't make it go away. How do you think Willow felt, knowing that her hearing was getting worse?

4. Willow, like us, could face problems with faith, or with her own strength. Like most of us, she flounders before she finds solid ground. When does Willow seem to let go and let God take over?

5. Clint returns home to take care of his ailing father, a man who has been abusive and neglectful. He realizes that although he's forgiven

his father, forgetting takes longer. How do we separate the two?

6. Clint's faith is strong, but he tries to take care of everyone in his life, and forgets that God is more than able to carry that burden. Have you ever found yourself in a similar situation? How did you handle it?

7. Clint's nephews spend a lot of time with Willow and Aunt Janie on their ranch. Do you think this was hard for Willow to handle, considering all she'd lost in her life? Why or why not?

8. Willow realizes that peace comes from God. The world, on the other hand, finds peace in possessions and in circumstances that go the way we want. How could Willow have dealt with her situation, other than seeking God? How did seeking God's peace change Willow's attitude toward her situation?

9. Clint sometimes confuses his need to "fix" people with love. What motivates that need to "fix" others? Are you guilty of trying to "fix" people? How?

10. Willow takes a chance and trusts Clint with her biggest secret, that she can't have children. How hard is it to open up in a relationship and let people know those things about ourselves that we could keep hidden?

11. When Clint learns that his sister has gone missing, he feels helpless, dependent on the strength of others, and dependent on God. Willow assures him that she can be strong for both of them. When have you been strong for others? How did the situation turn out?

12. When the church prays for Clint's sister, Jenna, to come home, the pastor teaches that prayer should be our first response, not an afterthought. "Just pray" takes on a new meaning when we realize that one definition of the word *just* is "immediately." If we realize the power of prayer, does it change our lives?

13. Willow prays for God to show her if Clint was the man who would love her forever. Did God show her Clint was the man for her? How? Have you ever asked for a sign from God? Was it answered? How?

*Turn the page for a sneak peek of*
*RITA® Award-winner Linda Goodnight's*
*heartwarming story,*
*HOME TO CROSSROADS RANCH.*
*On sale in March 2009*
*from Steeple Hill Love Inspired®*

## Chapter One

Nate Del Rio heard screams the minute he stepped out of his Ford F-150 SuperCrew and started up the flower-lined sidewalk leading to Rainy Jernagen's house. He doubled-checked the address scribbled on the back of a bill for horse feed. Sure enough, this was the place.

Adjusting his Stetson against a gust of March wind, he rang the doorbell, expecting the noise to subside. It didn't.

Somewhere inside the modest, tidy-looking brick house, at least two kids were screaming their heads off in what sounded to his experienced ears like fits of temper. A television blasted out Saturday morning cartoons—SpongeBob, he thought, though he was no expert on kids' television programs.

He punched the doorbell again. Instead of the expected *ding-dong,* a raucous alternative Christian rock band added a few more decibels to the noise level.

Nate shifted the toolbox to his opposite hand and considered running for his life while he had the chance.

Too late. The bright red door whipped open. Nate's mouth fell open with it.

When the men's ministry coordinator from Bible Fellowship had called him, he'd somehow gotten the impression that he was coming to help a little old school teacher. You know, the kind that only drives to school and church and has a big, fat cat.

Not so. The woman standing before him with taffy-blond hair sprouting out from a disheveled ponytail couldn't possibly be any older than his own thirty-one years. A big blotch of something purple stained the front of her white sweatshirt and she was barefooted. Plus, she had a crying baby on each hip and a little red-haired girl hanging on one leg, bawling like a sick calf. And there wasn't a cat in sight.

What had he gotten himself into?

"May I help you?" she asked over the racket. Her blue-gray eyes were a little too unfocused and bewildered for his comfort.

Raising his voice, he asked, "Are you Ms. Jernagen?"

"Yes," she said cautiously. "I'm Rainy Jernagen. And you are…?"

"Nate Del Rio."

She blinked, uncomprehending, all the while jiggling both babies up and down. One grabbed a hank of her hair. She flinched, her head angling to one side as she said, still cautiously, "Okaaay."

Nate reached out and untwined the baby's sticky fingers.

A relieved smile rewarded him. "Thanks. Is there something I can help you with?"

He hefted the red toolbox to chest level so she could see it. "From the Handy Man Ministry. Jack Martin called. Said you had a washer problem."

Understanding dawned. "Oh, my goodness. Yes. I'm so sorry. You aren't what I expected. Please forgive me."

She wasn't what he expected either. Not in the least. Young and with a houseful of kids. He suppressed a shiver. No wonder she looked like the north end of a southbound cow. Kids, even grown ones, could drive a person to distraction. He should know. His adult sister and brother were, at this moment, making his life as miserable as possible. The worst part was they did it all the time. Only this morning his sister, Janine, had finally packed up and gone back to Sal, giving Nate a few days' reprieve.

"Come in, come in," the woman was saying. "It's been a crazy morning what with the babies showing up at three a.m. and Katie having a sick stomach. Then while I was doing the laundry, the washing machine went crazy. Water everywhere." She jerked her chin toward the inside of the house. "You're truly a godsend."

He wasn't so sure about that, but he'd signed up for his church's ministry to help single women and the elderly with those pesky little handyman chores like oil changes and leaky faucets. Most of his visits had been to older ladies who plied him with sweet tea and jars of homemade jam and talked about the good old days while he replaced a fuse or unstopped the sink. And their houses had been quiet. Real quiet.

Rainy Jernagen stepped back, motioned him in, and Nate very cautiously entered a room that should have had flashing red lights and a *danger zone* sign.

Toys littered the living room like Christmas morning. An overturned cereal bowl flowed milk onto a coffee table. Next to a playpen crowding one wall, a green package belched out disposable diapers. Similarly, baby clothes were strewn, along with a couple of kids, on the couch and floor. In a word, the place was a wreck.

"The washer is back this way behind the kitchen. Watch your step. It's slippery."

More than slippery. Nate kicked his way through the living room and the kitchen area beyond, though the kitchen actually appeared much tidier than the rest, other than the slow seepage of water coming from somewhere beyond. The shine of liquid glistening on beige tile led them straight to the utility room.

"I turned the faucets off behind the washer when this first started, but a tubful still managed to pump out onto the floor." She hoisted the babies higher on her hip and spoke to a young boy sitting on the floor. "Joshua, get out of those suds."

"But they're pretty, Miss Rainy." The brown-haired boy with bright-blue eyes grinned up at her, extending a handful of bubbles. Light reflected off each droplet. "See the rainbows? There's always a rainbow, like you said. A rainbow behind the rain."

Miss Rainy smiled at the child. "Yes, there is. But right now, Mr. Del Rio needs in here to fix the washer. It's a little crowded for all of us." She was right about that. The space was no bigger than a small bathroom. "Can I get you to take the babies to the playpen while I show him around?"

"I'll take them, Miss Rainy." An older boy with a serious face and brown plastic glasses entered the room. Treading carefully, he came forward and took both babies, holding them against his slight chest. Another child appeared behind him. This one a girl with very blond hair and eyes the exact blue of the boy's, the one she'd called Joshua. How many children did this woman have, anyway? Six?

A heavy, smothery feeling pressed against his airway. Six kids?

Before he could dwell on that disturbing thought, a scream of sonic proportions rent the soap-fragrant air. He whipped around ready to protect and defend.

The little blond girl and the redhead were going at it.

"It's mine." Blondie tugged hard on a Barbie doll.

"It's mine. Will said so." To add emphasis to her demand, the redhead screamed bloody murder. "Miss Rainy."

About that time, Joshua decided to skate across the suds, and then slammed into the far wall next to a door that probably opened into the garage. He grabbed his big toe and set up a howl. Water sloshed as Rainy rushed forward and gathered him into her arms.

"Rainy!" Blondie screamed again.

"Rainy!" the redhead yelled.

Nate cast a glance at the garage exit and considered a fast escape.

*Lord, I'm here to do a good thing. Can you help me out a little?*

Rainy, her clothes now wet, somehow managed to take the doll from the fighting girls while snuggling Joshua against her side. The serious-looking boy stood in the doorway, a baby on each hip, taking in the chaos.

"Come on, Emma," the boy said to Blondie. "I'll make you some chocolate milk." So they went, slip-sliding out of the flooded room.

Four down, two to go.

Nate clunked his toolbox onto the washer and tried to ignore the chaos. Not an easy task, but one he'd learned to deal with as a boy. As an adult, he did everything possible to avoid this kind of madness. The Lord had a sense of humor sending him to this particular house.

"I apologize, Mr. Del Rio," Rainy said, shoving at the wads of hair that hung around her face like Spanish moss.

"Call me Nate. I'm not that much older than you." At thirty-one and the long-time patriarch of his family, he might feel seventy, but he wasn't.

"Okay, Nate. And I'm Rainy. Really, it's not usually

this bad. I can't thank you enough for coming over. I tried to get a plumber, but being Saturday…" she shrugged, letting the obvious go unsaid. No one could get a plumber on the weekend.

"No problem." He removed his white Stetson and placed it next to the toolbox. What was he supposed to say? That he loved wading in dirty soap suds and listening to kids scream and cry? Not likely.

Rainy stood with an arm around each of the remaining children—the rainbow boy and the redhead. Her look of embarrassment had him feeling sorry for her. All these kids and no man around to help. With this many, she'd never find another husband, he was sure of that. Who would willingly take on a boatload of kids?

After a minute, Rainy and the remaining pair left the room and he got to work. Wiggling the machine away from the wall wasn't easy. Even with all the water on the floor, a significant amount remained in the tub. This leftover liquid sloshed and gushed at regular intervals. In minutes, his boots were dark with moisture. No problem there. As a rancher, his boots were often dark with lots of things, the best of which was water.

On his haunches, he surveyed the back of the machine, where hoses and cords and metal parts twined together like a nest of water moccasins.

As he investigated each hose in turn, he once more felt a presence in the room. Pivoting on his heels, he discovered the two boys squatted beside him, attention glued to the back of the washer.

"A busted hose?" the oldest one asked, pushing up his glasses.

"Most likely."

"I coulda fixed it but Rainy wouldn't let me."

"That so?"

"Yeah. Maybe. If someone would show me."

Nate suppressed a smile. "What's your name?"

"Will. This here's my brother, Joshua." He yanked a thumb at the younger one. "He's nine. I'm eleven. You go to Miss Rainy's church?"

"I do, but it's a big church. I don't think we've met before."

"She's nice. Most of the time. She never hits us or anything, and we've been here for six months."

It occurred to Nate then that these were not Rainy's children. The kids called her Miss Rainy, not Mom, and according to Will they had not been here forever. But what was a young, single woman doing with all these kids?

\* \* \* \* \*

*Look for*
*HOME TO CROSSROADS RANCH*
*by Linda Goodnight,*
*on sale March 2009 only from*
*Steeple Hill Love Inspired®,*
*available wherever books are sold.*

# *Love Inspired®*
# SUSPENSE
### RIVETING INSPIRATIONAL ROMANCE

Watch for our new series of
edge-of-your-seat suspense novels.
These contemporary tales
of intrigue and romance
feature Christian characters
facing challenges to their faith...
and their lives!

**Steeple
Hill®**

Visit:
**www.SteepleHill.com**

LISUSDIR07R

**INSPIRATIONAL HISTORICAL ROMANCE**

Engaging stories of romance,
adventure and faith,
these novels are set in
various historical periods
from biblical times
to World War II.

## NOW AVAILABLE!

**Steeple
Hill®**

For exciting stories that reflect traditional values,
visit:
**www.SteepleHill.com**